He didn't let go of her at once

He went on holding her, looking into her face as though he planned on doing a sketch from memory. He grinned. "What would your boyfriend do if he knew you were stuck out here with me?"

Pattie shrugged. "If he did know, what could he do, if even a snowplough can't get through?" Duncan seemed to be condsidering, and she asked dryly, "What would you do? Drop in by helicopter or swoop down on skis?"

"One or the other."

Pattie believed him, and she felt a stab of jealousy. "Who would you pluck out of here?"

He shook his head at her, smiling, and she was glad. She didn't want a name. She didn't want to hear about the woman he would come rushing to rescue.

Books by Jane Donnelly

HARLEQUIN ROMANCES

These books may be available at your local bookseller.

For a list of all titles currently available,
send your name and address to:

Harlequin Reader Service
P.O. Box 52040, Phoenix, AZ 85072-2040
Canadian address: P.O. Box 2800, Postal Station A,
5170 Yonge St., Willowdale, Ont. M2N 5T5

The Frozen Heart

Jane Donnelly

Harlequin Books

TORONTO • NEW YORK • LONDON
AMSTERDAM • PARIS • SYDNEY • HAMBURG
STOCKHOLM • ATHENS • TOKYO • MILAN

Original hardcover edition published in 1981
by Mills & Boon Limited

ISBN 0-373-02654-4

Harlequin Romance first edition November 1984

CHAPTER ONE

THE photograph made her choke over her coffee. The coffee was hot, just perked, and Pattie Ross had been sipping when she turned to the gossip page in her morning paper and saw the fair-haired girl, on the arm of a man, smiling. Then she took in a great scalding gulp that made her gasp and splutter and brought tears to her eyes.

'Romance is in the air again,' announced the caption coyly, 'for 23-year-old Jennifer Stanley whose wedding to Nigel Poynton, son of millionaire landowner Lord Poynton, was called off a year ago, with the invitations out and the bride's dress made. At the time the lovely Jennifer was terribly distressed, so it is good to see her happy again with her new fiancé, librarian Wilfred Jarvis.'

It certainly is good, thought Pattie. She had never met Jennifer Stanley, but she had played a part in that wedding cancellation. All in a day's work, everybody had said. Well, no, not everybody—all her colleagues and most of her friends—but Pattie had felt guilty at the way her small scoop had turned out. It had influenced her life as well as Jennifer's. She had been offered a job on a magazine just before, she had been considering it, and shortly after Jennifer Stanley was left in the lurch Pattie Ross had resigned from her newspaper post and gone to work on a women's magazine.

She had never admitted even to herself that the

Jennifer Stanley story had tipped the balance of her decision. But seeing the photograph brought back some very unpleasant memories.

It *was* good to see that Jennifer Stanley had found happiness, but rather ironic for this to be appearing in the column that had caused her so much public humiliation and hurt. The man looked nice and Pattie wished them well, and turned the page and finished drinking her coffee, and skimming the news, in the ten minutes she allowed herself for breakfast each morning.

She was a well-organised girl. She washed her coffee cup and saucer and made her bed before she left, as she always did. She never came back from the office to an untidy flat, even if she had entertained late in the night before. She did the chores automatically, then slipped into her camel trench coat and picked up tan gloves and tan shoulder-strapped holdall.

In the mirror by the door she made an attractive picture. She was slim, her dark hair fell round her face in smooth wings from a centre parting. Her face was oval, her features were regular and her skin was lightly tanned from a weekly solarium session.

She looked exactly as she expected to look, and wanted to look, a successful career girl; but today she found that she was frowning. She had woken feeling unsettled. She could have understood it if it had been spring, that was a restless season although Pattie had never done anything really crazy even in springtime. It was winter now, cold and bleak in the world outside, but she did have one small problem, and maybe that was unsettling her.

She was starting a holiday this afternoon, she had

two weeks owing to her. Michael Ames, her boy-friend, was a chartered accountant and he was off to the Cotswolds to see various clients, staying in a comfortable hotel. If Pattie went too she could laze around, take walks, spend evenings with Michael and friends he had down there. That had been the arrangement until a few days ago when she had looked around her flat and decided it was in a desperate need of freshening up.

Michael said he couldn't see it. The oyster white walls of the living room looked like new to him, and Michael was as fastidious as Pattie herself. They were very alike. People remarked that they even looked alike and asked if they were related. When they first met, six months ago at a party, they had found that their tastes coincided in all manner of ways. It had been lovely. Everything they talked about they agreed on, and they had stayed together all evening as though they couldn't bear to lose sight of each other. Except for a few minutes when Michael went to the bar and Pattie overheard a girl say, 'Michael's been in love with himself for years and now he's found a mirror image,' and a man chortled, 'Remember what happened to Mick Jagger?' Pattie hadn't repeated that to Michael. She hadn't realised till then that they looked like brother and sister, and since that party she and Michael had developed a very satisfactory relationship.

She admired him tremendously. He was very good at his job and Pattie liked that, she liked efficiency; and he was always elegant, perfectly turned out, and she found that reassuring, because she had a horror of scruffiness. Her friends approved of him and his mother said that Pattie was a charming girl.

She couldn't have faulted Michael on anything. They rarely argued and they never rowed, and although he was put out at first, about Pattie stopping behind to paint her flat, he finally admitted that perhaps there were cooking fumes on the kitchen ceiling. Professional decorators cost the earth these days and if Pattie wanted to do it herself it was her holiday and her apartment. He didn't offer to help when they got back, he never got his hands dirty.

So she would be buying paint this afternoon, and spending the next week applying it to the walls, when she could have been sitting by great log fires and dining off haute cuisine food. With Michael with her all the time he was not with clients. He had stressed that his schedule allowed plenty of leisure and if she changed her mind it had to be before midday, because he had to leave at twelve.

The flat didn't look bad. It was immaculate by most standards, although new coats of paint would lighten it a little. Pattie stood looking around at the cool colours: whites, greys, pale pastel blue in the bedroom, and wondered how it would be if she filled one wall with a sunburst paper or painted it geranium red, and smiled at herself because it would be completely out of character. It wouldn't go with her, it wouldn't go with the furniture.

I'll go with Michael, she decided. I'll look in at the office, then come back and pack a bag. Perhaps it's a break I need, a change. She pushed aside the thought that the Cotswold jaunt would mean a change of scene and a change of food, but being with Michael would be like reading a book she knew by heart. There would be no surprises there . . . .

Pattie's desk in the Features Department where

she worked was clear. The other desks in the room were usually cluttered, but she worked better among order, and as she was starting her holiday today she had made a particular effort to leave no loose ends.

The article she had finished yesterday was on the features editor's desk and Roz Rickard, features editor, was trying out a new blusher, squinting sidewards at herself in a mirror propped up against her husband's photograph. She was a redhead, with smoky blue eyes that looked shortsighted and vague, but in fact she was sharp as a needle.

'Do you like the colour?' she asked Pattie.

It looked like a purplish bruise and Pattie looked doubtful, and Roz shrugged, 'I didn't buy it. It's one of Dinah's.' Dinah was the beauty editor, new cosmetics of all sorts and shades were constantly arriving for her department. 'Not me, I think,' said Roz. 'Well, are you off to the Cotswolds?'

Pattie hesitated. 'I don't know.'

'Go on,' urged Roz. 'Go and have some fun, Michael's a poppet.' She wiped off the blusher streak with a cleanser pad, and added mischievously, 'Not a riot, but a poppet.'

'Who wants a riot?' said Pattie, and for some reason the image of her living room wall came into her mind, in a riot of bright jungle colours, although she knew that she could never live with that kind of wallpaper. She shivered a little and put her hands on the radiator. Pattie had the desk by the radiator, she felt the cold more than most, but today it was bitter and the walk from her space in the car park to the entrance to the building had chilled her to the bone. 'How is it?' she asked, nodding towards her article.

'Fine,' said Roz. 'Yes, super. Although perhaps

we're overdoing the happy families.'

Pattie did a regular feature called 'Man of the Month', interviewing men whom her readers would have liked to meet. Glamorous, handsome, successful men. Most of them were in show business, and all of them were eager to be interviewed because it was good publicity. The photographs accompanying the article were always flattering, and Pattie always turned in a story that made the reader feel she was there, being chatted up by the month's charmer.

It wasn't as easy as that, of course. Pattie was a good interviewer. She asked the questions and guided the talk, and when it came to putting it down on paper cut out the waffle so that they all sounded intelligent and witty and stimulating, although some of them had been thick as two planks.

This one she had quite enjoyed. He was an actor and an amusing talker. He had made her smile and she was fairly sure the readers would chuckle with her, and there were some delightful shots of him taken with his blonde wife and two small blonde children.

The phone rang on Roz's desk. She answered and held it towards Pattie. 'Can I help you?' said Pattie.

'What did you have in mind, dear?' said a male voice that she recognised so that her expression became wry while he went on to ask, 'Have you read the column this morning?'

Willie Dyson meant his column. He really didn't believe there was any other. He was the gossip-writer and Pattie had been on his team before she came here. She quite liked Willie, although he was a malicious little man, but she was very glad she didn't work with him any more.

'Yes,' she said.

'The Jennifer Stanley story?'

'Oh yes.'

'Nice little follow-up, wasn't it?' he said smugly. 'It's just twelve months since the wedding was called off,' and Pattie gasped. 'You'll see that the Honourable Nigel wished her well,' Willie chattered on. 'We tried to get a quote from Duncan Keld all day yesterday, but we couldn't get hold of him. Nice to know everything's turned out all right, isn't it? She's a pretty little thing.'

'You have the hide of a rhinoceros!' shrieked Pattie, making Roz sit up and take notice, and as Willie protested in injured tones she put down the phone.

'And what was that all about?' asked Roz.

'This.' Pattie produced her morning paper, unfolded it and turned to Willie's page, pointing to the photograph. 'Remember her?'

'Ye—es,' Roz read, with furrowed brow.

She knew the background. Jennifer Stanley was a devastatingly pretty but priggish girl who had nearly married the son of a multi-millionaire. The forthcoming wedding had received some press coverage and Jennifer kept on talking about waiting for Mr Right, and insisting there had never been a man in her life before the Honourable Nigel Poynton. So that when a girl sitting by Pattie in the Birmingham to London express said she had worked with Jennifer, for a few weeks the year before last, Pattie listened without revealing that she was a journalist.

A sketch of Jennifer's wedding dress was on the women's page of a morning paper that day and Jennifer was stressing that she was wearing pure white, and asking scornfully how many brides were entitled to do that these days, and Pattie's travelling companion said, 'She isn't, for one. All this holier-than-thou stuff!'

It was a freaky thing to happen, a chance meeting in a million, and Pattie suspected that the girl was spinning a line, but next morning she mentioned it at the editorial conference. 'I don't suppose there's any truth in this, but I met a girl yesterday who said that Jennifer Stanley, who's getting married next week, once had an affair with Duncan Keld.'

'With *who*?' Willie had squeaked, his little eyes gleaming.

'Yes, that one,' said Pattie. 'A girl I met on the train works in this bookshop, where she said Jennifer had a summer job when she was down from college, and he was signing books there.'

'Which bookshop?' Willie demanded, and Pattie told him.

'She said that Jennifer went overboard for him. She cleared off, night after night. It petered out when he went back up north, he's got a house in Yorkshire, she said, but it was the real thing—I mean it was a real affair.'

Duncan Keld was well known, his books and his photograph got big displays, he appeared on TV and his articles were printed in the heavier newspapers. But he was enough of a rogue figure to make the idea of him and Jennifer Stanley intriguing. Willie liked it. He set about checking. Duncan Keld was abroad, nobody knew exactly where, but all Willie had to do was mention his name and the date to Jennifer and she croaked, 'Oh, my God, no!' and began to threaten what would happen if they linked her name with his in any way. No, she said—no, he was not invited to the wedding, but well yes, all right, she had met him. Yes, she supposed they had in a way been friends.

So Willie ran a paragraph: 'Missing from the guest list at next week's society wedding of 28-year-old Nigel Poynton to stunning blonde beauty Jennifer Stanley is best-seller writer Duncan Keld. Strange that, as not so long ago the lovely Jennifer and Keld were very good friends. Maybe Nigel vetted the list.'

The next thing was that the wedding was off, presents were being returned and it was announced that both Nigel and Jennifer had had last-minute second thoughts. A week later Willie's car hit a tree. At least that was his story when he arrived at the office with a black eye and a puffy countenance and he stuck to it, but all his colleagues knew that Duncan Keld had been looking for him and there wasn't a scratch on the car. And a few days after that, when Pattie was eating her lunch in a pub round the corner from the office with several workmates, the man sitting next to her whistled, 'Stewth, it's Keld!' and she turned to see this huge dark figure bearing down on them.

He was a big man and as he came through the chattering crowds he seemed to Pattie as menacing as though he carried a gun. He made straight for her and stood looking down at her and said, 'Pattie Ross?' and she nodded soundlessly. Nobody else said a word. Everybody who knew him and her waited to see what was going to happen next, and then he said, 'I wanted to get a good look at you,' and he smiled. Pattie was scared to death—then he said almost gently, 'Thank your lucky stars you're a woman or I'd have blacked your eyes too.'

He knew she was the one who had come up with the story, but what he didn't know, of course, was that she wished she hadn't. It must have caused so much unhappiness and it made her realise that she hadn't the stomach for this kind of journalism.

She never regretted changing jobs. Roz was as astute as Willie and kinder. Now Roz looked up from the picture of Jennifer Stanley and her new fiancé and said, 'Quite a coincidence, because I've been thinking about him.'

The new fiancé? Pattie looked puzzled and Roz said, 'Duncan Keld. He's got a TV series in the summer. He'd make a good Man of the Month.'

Pattie gulped, 'You mean you want me to interview him?'

'Why not? I know he had it in for you over this business, but he's probably forgotten all about it by now and he's got all the qualifications we need. Our readers would love a date with him.'

'I wouldn't,' said Pattie.

'Why not?'

Pattie had no choice, she took the assignments she was given, but Roz was listening and she was hard put to explain how threatened she had felt when he came across that room looking for her. She shook her head. 'I don't like him. I don't like rough tough men.'

'You don't know what you're missing,' Roz grinned, and Pattie said,

'He might not want to talk to me.'

If he did she thought it would be a difficult session. She couldn't imagine him co-operating as the others had done, anxious to make a good impression and get a good write-up. Roz was telling her, 'Look on him as a challenge. A touch of antagonism wouldn't hurt. Go for one who can be mean and moody for a change.'

'You've just thought of this, haven't you?' said Pattie, and Roz admitted gleefully,

'Yes—and I wonder I didn't think of him before. Rough, tough, successful and sexy is a lovely combination.'

Pattie gave a deep sigh. 'Well, I'm certainly glad I'm on holiday. I shall need at least a week in a good hotel to get my strength up if I'm due to start tracking Duncan Keld as soon as I get back.'

She was making the best of it and trying to joke, but she hated the idea. He couldn't have forgotten what she had done. Even if he was no longer angry he would still in all probability tell her to get lost, and then she would have to admit to Roz that this was an interview she couldn't deliver. That would make Roz even keener so that she might send someone else along, or go herself, and it would be a mark of failure against Pattie.

She was proud of her reputation for reliability. 'You can depend on Pattie,' her friends always said, and she was lucky that this was the first unpleasant assignment she had been given since she started here. It had all been smooth going, hard work but no hassles, and perhaps some of these Man of the Month articles had been a little cloying. Duncan Keld wasn't Pattie's idea of the man she would like to date, but Roz, who was happy and faithful in her marriage, had drooled over him. So, in the month the serialisation of his book started on TV, an article about him would appear, and with luck it would carry Pattie's byline.

She went downstairs to the library to get out the envelope with his name on, as she always did before she interviewed celebrities. By the time she met them she aimed on knowing as much as possible about them, and hers wouldn't be the first interview by a long way that had been written about Duncan Keld.

There were plenty of photographs too. She sat at one of the green-leather-topped tables, with the cuttings spread out before her, and he seemed to be looking back at her from every picture. He had dark eyes that photographed piercingly, but Pattie found her own eyes sliding away from the pictures and concentrating on the print.

There was the small gossip column paragraph linking his name with Jennifer Stanley dated this month last year, and she put that quickly back into the envelope. He got around. All over the world, going by this lot, mostly in the trouble spots. He had a flat in London and a hunting lodge on the Yorkshire moors. There was a photograph of him outside the lodge, hair ruffled by the wind, laughing. The black and white hills would have been purple and green—Pattie knew that place. She had never been to the lodge, of course, but she had had it pointed out to her across the hills during a motoring holiday in Yorkshire last summer, and it was such beautiful countryside.

'Heathcliff with a Sense of Humour' ran the headline to the article and Glenda, one of the girls in the library, giggled, passing the table and looking at the photograph, 'I wouldn't kick him out of bed!'

'Oh, *you*!' said Pattie, pretending to be shocked. Glenda was a pert and pretty teenager who tried hard to sound blasé and shocking, but although she smiled Pattie's stomach muscles clenched in distaste. Her instinctive reaction to 'Heathcliff with a Sense of Humour' had been 'Yeuk!'

She made a list of his books and his TV plays, and took notes of tastes, opinions and background and his London address and phone number. Then she returned the envelope to its place on the shelves, and everybody wished her a nice holiday, and she went down to the car park and her little white Mini.

She bought two of Duncan Keld's paperbacks on her way home. She never had read any of his books, but she had seen some of the TV adaptations and he could tell a story. The characters lived and the action raced, she would give him that, and if the weather stayed this cold she would be sitting by the hotel fire rather than wandering around the streets and lanes of the small town. She would need some reading matter.

She had missed the post this morning. Sometimes it arrived just before she left, often afterwards, and there was an airmail from her mother lying on the mat when she opened the door. She turned on a bar of the electric fire, and sat down in front of it to read her letter. Everything was all right. Her mother was leading the pleasant life that suited her, and described a few outings and a new silk suit she had bought the day before she wrote the letter. She sent her love, and the love of Pattie's stepfather. 'And give my love to Michael,' wrote Pattie's mother, who had spoken to Michael on the phone and learned about him through Pattie's letters. 'And when are you going to get around to thinking about marrying him, because he sounds just perfect for you. So don't let him get away.'

Her mother would like her married. She and her husband would fly over for the ceremony, although he was a busy doctor, and the ones who hadn't met her before would be astonished when they saw Pattie's mother. 'She's got to be your sister,' they'd say. She did look young, but she didn't look like Pattie. Michael was the one who looked like Pattie, and one day soon they were going to think about getting married. They had discussed it. He hadn't proposed exactly, but they talked about a future together, and he had dropped hints about Pattie having an engagement ring for her birthday at the beginning of May.

It was the end of January now and if Michael did produce a ring she supposed she would accept it. She packed her mother's letter, not to show Michael but to answer during the next few days, and then the clothes she would need for her little holiday. Packing didn't take long. Her clothes were always bandbox fresh, and she rang the paper shop to cancel her paper, and switched off switches, then got out of London on to the M40 heading for Gloucestershire.

At this time of year she was sure she would be able to book into the hotel where Michael was staying. He might have booked for her anyway, he'd thought there was a chance she might come. She would be arriving several hours late but before dinner, so that should be all right, and she found the hotel without having to ask directions, in the main road opposite the church.

She didn't know why she didn't mention Michael's name. She had meant to ask, 'Has Mr Ames arrived?' He should have done, unless he'd called on a client first, but instead she asked, 'Have you a single room?'

and booked herself in, signing the register several lines beneath Michael's neat sloping writing.

The single room was warm, impersonal but adequate, and Pattie unpacked and changed into a dress in soft blue jersey. She wore very small pearl ear-studs and a medallion on a long chain. The surround of white onyx was inset with gold filigree and Chinese symbols representing health and happiness. All her jewellery was genuine, and usually small and neat, but this medallion was her favourite. She would have traded all the rest in for this. It was the only piece that really mattered.

She would go down to the lounge fifteen minutes or so before dinner and see if Michael was there. He would be pleased to see her. If he was late she would try to get a table in the restaurant where she could watch the door, and she smiled and told herself what fun the surprise would be. That was why she hadn't identified herself, because she wanted to surprise him. 'Serve you right,' Roz would have said, 'if he's brought another woman,' but Pattie had no fear of that. She knew Michael and she trusted him as he trusted her.

She took extra care with her make-up, and dabbed on his favourite scent. It was her choice too. She always bought it, and he had recognised it and said how much he liked it. 'But of course,' she had smiled at him. 'Isn't that how it always happens? If I'd been choosing you a tie I'd have selected the one you're wearing.'

I'm getting ready to meet my lover, she thought, breathing in the soft sweet perfume on the pulse point of her wrist, so why isn't my heart racing? She frowned at her reflection in the mirror over the dressing table, as she had frowned this morning, with the same sensation of flatness. There wasn't a thing wrong with her life. She loved her job, she loved Michael, but if she loved Michael why didn't she feel excited about going down and surprising him and having dinner with him and being with him?

Perhaps it was the weather. She really hated the winter. Perhaps it was blunting her feelings, because usually she enjoyed being with Michael. And she needed her dinner. She would choose something absolutely delicious from the menu and she and Michael would have a feast.

He wasn't in the lounge, which was full of armchairs covered in green cabbage-rose chintz, with a beamed ceiling and the big log fire she had been promised. The middle-aged men and women sitting around looked as though they were mainly here on winter bargain breaks, and Pattie got several admiring and enquiring glances as an elegant girl alone.

After one man with a very red face and a prodigious waistline tried to chat her up she took out Duncan Keld's book and started to read. She looked less aimless that way, and from the first paragraph she was hooked. He was very, very good, and when she looked up again a waiter was hovering with a menu and she realised the time was passing, and the lounge was almost empty.

She ordered and took her seat. The dining room was about half full, but Michael wasn't there, and that probably meant that he was eating somewhere else. She should have got in touch. She could at least have rung before he left and said she was following, although even while she was packing she had still been undecided. It would have taken hardly anything to make her change her mind again. And yet she wasn't usually a ditherer.

She could see the door from where she sat, and she saw Michael come in with two other men when she was nearing the end of her meal. He didn't see her, and when they reached their table he took a chair that meant he had his back to her, and he and his companions went on talking business.

She couldn't hear them, they were at the other end of the room, but their gestures and expressions had all the signs of amiable discussion, and she looked at Michael's shoulders and the back of his head and thought, he hasn't a clue I'm here.

There was no reason why he should have, unless he'd looked in the register, and it was stupid to feel resentful because he didn't know when she was near. If it had been the other way round and he had been waiting, and she had walked into a room, not looking for him and not expecting him, she wouldn't have sensed his presence either. Worse than that, now that she did see him she had no urge to go over to him. And it wasn't because they were talking business and she was reluctant to interrupt. It was because nothing was calling to her.

He would be pleased to see her, he had wanted her to come, but surely she should be feeling more than this? It was as though seeing him was like the meal she had just eaten, pleasant, satisfying. She had only said goodbye to him yesterday, but she wasn't hungry for him and she never would be. If she didn't see him for years she would never starve from want-ing him, and perhaps that meant she was incapable of real passion. She hadn't thought about it before. At twenty-two she had believed she was happy, but the underlying restlessness of the last few days suddenly centred on Michael Ames' unknowing head.

If I'm bored with him now, she thought, what would it be like in ten years' time? What would it be like being married to him? She left the dining room, and half her cheese and biscuits, and went up to her room. She was thankful she had booked herself in. She could leave in the morning, he need never know she was here, and when Michael returned she would try to find a kindly way of suggesting they should see rather less of each other.

This wasn't Michael's fault. How could she complain that a man bored her when he had the same tastes she had, and most of the same opinions? That had to mean she was boring too, and perhaps she was. Sitting alone in the dining room she had suddenly felt brittle and bloodless, as though she had settled for second-best all her life, and unless she did something pretty drastic, pretty soon, that was all she was ever going to get.

She couldn't see herself making any big dramatic gestures, she was too inhibited for that. She couldn't change her job, she loved it, but she might change her decor, and paper that wall in her apartment in jungle colours.

She realised she was clutching the gold and onyx medallion on its thin golden chain, and that showed her how confused she was, because at one time in moments of stress she had held on to that like a talisman. Once she wore it night and day, but in recent years only when it suited her outfit, and now here she was with it pressed tight between her clasped hands.

She had dropped her handbag and paperback on the bed and she looked down at Duncan Keld's book and said, 'You haven't helped any.' She was supposed to be a writer herself, but his work was immeasurably better than hers, which was rather depressing. In the pages she had read before dinner the fictional characters had seemed more alive than most of the living people she knew, and she resolved to do her very best to get that interview with him.

She still didn't like him, but that had nothing to do with it, and Roz could be right, the Man of the Month could be getting too cosy. This time perhaps Pattie could produce a really thrilling character study.

She hardly ever acted on impulse, but now she sat down on the bed and picked up the phone and asked for Duncan Keld's number. She wouldn't say who she was. Unless he enquired she would just give the name of her magazine, and ask if they might come along and get a story to coincide with his TV serial. He wouldn't know her voice because she'd never spoken to him, and if he remembered her when he saw her—well, she'd cross that bridge later.

The phone rang and she waited, still holding her health and happiness medallion because she needed to be lucky. But the man's voice sounded older and it wasn't Duncan Keld. He was sorry, but Mr Keld was away, he would be for several weeks, and Pattie grimaced and asked,

'I suppose you couldn't give me another number? It's rather urgent.'

'Mr Keld is in Yorkshire and not on the telephone.'

'At the lodge?'

There was a slight hesitation, then the voice admitted, 'That is correct,' and Pattie thanked him.

She was nearly halfway there. Nobody was expecting her back in London and she didn't want to stay here. She had friends up north, or she could put up in small hotels, and if she turned up on Duncan Keld's doorstep in the middle of the Yorkshire moors surely he would let her in. He'd only looked at her for about a minute twelve months ago, and she didn't have the kind of face that men remembered. It was all right, but there was nothing outstanding about it. Besides, even if he did recognise her Jennifer Stanley was looking happy again now.

Roz had said this was a challenge, and seeing if she could land Duncan Keld would be more exciting than returning home and decorating her apartment, no matter what wallpaper she selected.

Of course she might feel different in the morning, and go down and have breakfast with Michael, and tell him she hadn't joined his table last night because she'd realised he was with business colleagues, not because she simply hadn't wanted to. She would sleep on it. And she did. But she woke still sure of one thing: she wasn't breakfasting with Michael.

She had breakfast in her room and came out about ten o'clock when he should have left. But she still moved warily. She would feel an idiot if he caught her creeping down the stairs, or settling the bill, or of course he could have seen her car in the car park—and that stopped her in her tracks.

But there was no sign of Michael, and no note in her cubbyhole, and she drove out of town feeling quite pleased with herself.

She was a good driver, and she had only had the

car serviced a few weeks earlier so it was going well. It looked very cold outside. Iron-grey was the pervading colour. The sky was unbroken and heavy, and colours of houses and people all seemed to have merged into greyness. But it was warm in the car and Pattie played cassettes. There were too many news bulletins on the radio, and although she was travelling this way on work she was actually on holiday, and she could do without gloomy headlines.

She sang softly to herself with the singers, and made good time reaching the village where she had stayed last summer. She had an excellent memory for places. Like her sense of direction it was almost photographic. Once Pattie had covered a route she seemed to file it somewhere in her head, and she had no doubts about being able to find that hunting lodge, which was about six miles over the moors.

But summer and winter had different aspects. This little town, which had glowed in mellow sunshine, now looked shuttered and alien, and her new impulsiveness took over again. Driving conditions weren't too bad yet, but that sky was threatening. Once she stopped at the small hotel, where she had stayed previously, she was going to be loath to turn out again today. She remembered where the lodge was, but another half hour's driving would pinpoint it for her, so that tomorrow, even if there should be snow, she would know exactly how to reach it. Then, in the morning, she would return and knock on the door and try to make her peace with Duncan Keld.

It was all very different from the last time she had driven along here with three other girls. The road, winding between the glowering hills, had the same twists and turns, but the hills were darker. She passed a farm, ticking it off in her mind, some sheep huddled together. The trees were black and bare edging the road and when she turned off on to a track, climbing higher, no trees grew, and she could feel the wind beating against the door panels of the car.

She could see the lodge, squatting on the hillside, with smoke spiralling out of the chimney, and she kept going. She might knock now, and chance her luck while she felt lucky. She was in a state bordering on euphoria, as though she had done something daring and clever, and in that moment the end nearly came.

She was watching the lodge instead of the track so that she didn't see the patch of smooth ice, and her wheels had locked and her car had slithered over the unwalled edge before she could make any attempt to get out of the skid. The car went completely out of control, bouncing down what seemed to be a precipice and was a fairly steep hill, and although her seat-belt held her she felt as though she was being shaken to death. Then it began to roll, over and over, and her world became a nightmare kaleidoscope, splintered and screaming, and she knew she was going to die. She screamed and beat the air and the tumbling metal box that was taking her with it down into hell.

Then she was rocking, shaking, but not falling any more, and she thought she could smell petrol and remembered the flaming end of falling cars on TV and began to fumble with her seat-belt, sobbing and praying, her fingers without feeling. Somehow the clasp sprung loose, and she tried a jammed door and then another that gave, and clambered out on top of the car and jumped and began running.

She didn't look where she was going. She just ran before the car exploded, climbing higher, getting away from it. She didn't stop to think she might have broken any bones. She hadn't, but a sprained ankle wouldn't have stopped her. She was paranoid with panic, and she didn't stop at all until she was at the top of the hill, then she fell to her knees and slithered face down, fingers clutching the coarse frozen grass, heaving her heart out.

She had never been so close to death. She was in deep shock, whimpering like a puppy, and finally raised her head and looked around with dazed eyes.

She saw the car below. It hadn't exploded, but it had fallen a long way, and it lay on its side, the white paintwork scarred and dented, and it began to dawn on her how lucky she had been. She could have been dead. She could have been horribly injured, lying where no one might find her for days.

She clambered up the hill, but now she began moving her arms and legs slowly, stretching this way and that, unable to believe that she was comparatively unhurt. There was no blood, and no bones seemed to be broken. Ahead the smoke still rose from the lodge chimney and she began to stumble towards it, sobbing, but now from relief.

On foot it seemed a long way. The wind was icy, and when she reached the greystone building with its heavy wooden door she was so exhausted that she could hardly summon the strength to knock. She leaned against the door, her frosted breath rising. She couldn't shout, it would have come out in a whisper, but she did bang her fist, slowly and as hard as she could.

Then she closed her eyes and waited. Nobody

came. She beat on the door again, waited again, then she made herself shout, 'Hello. Anybody there? Hello!'

The silence was unbroken, and a boost of adrenalin gave her energy enough to bang with both hands and yell good and loud. There was a fire in there. Somebody had to be home. Somebody had to answer. But nobody did, and she tried to peer in through the windows.

It was dark inside, except for the flicker of firelight, and she kept up her calls of 'Hello', tapping the window panes, stumbling round the house, to the back where she almost fell over a great log pile.

He would be coming back, because the fire was burning, but if nobody helped her soon she was going to catch pneumonia at the very least. More probably freeze to death because—oh, God, it was starting to snow. Little feathery flakes were floating down, tangling in her eyelashes, although she couldn't feel them on her face or her hands because her skin was as cold as the snow.

She had to get inside. Front and back doors were locked, so she would have to smash a window. There had to be something she could smash the glass with, but as she tapped on a small window it moved slightly and she pushed, and it wasn't latched.

She had been wrong believing she was at the end of her tether when she reached the lodge. She had reserves enough left to haul herself up and wriggle herself in through the narrow aperture. She landed on a sink, and this was shelter even if the door of the room was locked. She could huddle in here until help came. But the latch lifted and the door swung open and in an inglenook fireplace logs smouldered, and she ran towards them crowing with delight.

She didn't move for a long time. She stayed in the blessed circle of warmth, until the blood was prickling painfully in her veins and she had to rub the circulation back. When she stood up she was trembling and she held on to the arm of a chair while she looked round the room.

A very big room, almost the whole of the ground floor; rugs on flagstones, easy chairs and an old table. But she was in no state to notice the furniture, and she went to a door that opened on to a staircase and called, 'Is anybody up there?' although if there was they were either deaf or dead.

She really had the shakes. She would have given pounds for a cup of strong sweet tea. She had landed in the kitchen, where there was a Calor gas stove, but she didn't know how to turn it on, and she daren't trust herself to balance a kettle on the logs.

Then she saw the bottles on a dresser. One was brandy, and if ever she had needed a brandy for her health's sake she needed one now. It splashed when she poured, she could hardly hold the bottle, but she finally got a good measure into the glass and added a little soda water, then carried it back to the fire.

As soon as she had moved away from the direct heat she had felt cold again, which showed she was still in shock, and now she huddled down in a massive old armchair in front of the fire, pulling a rug over her.

She had never taken a drink this strong before. It scalded her throat and made her head swim before she was half way through it, but she gulped it down and within minutes she was asleep.

She could have slept till morning. She was in deep

slumber when she was woken, so that she opened heavy eyes and stared stupidly, still slightly drugged by the brandy.

He could have been part of a bad dream—big, looming over her. Her head ached, she was aching everywhere, and she was still slowly and painfully regaining consciousness when she heard him say in a harsh voice that went through her brain like a buzz-saw, 'How in hell did you get in here?' and before she could answer, 'Never mind how, just get out!'

CHAPTER TWO

'I CAN'T go anywhere,' Pattie croaked. 'My car crashed.'

He showed no sympathy. He just went on glowering down at her, and as she raised her head pain stabbed so that she winced and he said, 'Sure it isn't a hangover?'

The empty glass was beside her. The way her hands had been shaking when she'd poured it out she could have spilled some of the brandy down her, she could be reeking of the stuff. She said stiffly, 'Sorry, do let me pay for it, but I was shaken up. I ran my car off the track and I climbed in through a back window to get to the fire.'

'With anyone else,' he drawled, 'I'd say you're welcome.'

He had recognised her. She wouldn't have thought she looked at all like her usual self, and the light was dim—fireglow, and there seemed to be a lamp somewhere—but maybe he remembered faces the way she did places. She remembered his face all right. Except that if anything he looked even grimmer than the last time.

She began, 'I'm Pattie Ross——' and he cut in,

'I know who you are. What I'm waiting to be told is what you're doing here.'

The lodge was a long way off the road. If Pattie had been taking the track there was nowhere else she could have been heading but here, and she hadn't the strength to be conciliatory. She could only blurt, 'I want to interview you.'

'You *what?*' He laughed derisively. 'I'd rather be interviewed by the K.G.B.!'

She couldn't deal with this. She leaned back and said wearily, 'In that case I'll have to trouble you to drive me into Grimslake,' and for a moment she thought he would strike her. He was obviously seething with anger, and it was dark and the drive would be an unpleasant one, and what was she going to do if he took her to the hotel? She had no luggage and no money. Everything was down there in the car. In the morning she could retrieve her belongings, so she asked hesitantly, 'Or could I stay the night?'

He glared at her from under beetling brows. 'You'll bloody well have to stay the night.'

'Thank you,' she said, and he snarled,

'Save your breath, I've got no choice.' He looked as though he wanted to smash something, preferably her, and she said meekly, 'I'll stay here, shall I?' The chair was no bed. It was lumpy. But there was no need for him to carry on as though she was going to disrupt everything. Of course she could sleep in the chair.

'There's one bed upstairs,' he said. 'Mine. You're not suggesting we share it?' And he looked at her with a blistering contempt that made her curl up, and brought hot colour to her cheeks. He was a swine—but before she could tell him so he had marched off, picked up the lamp, and vanished through the door to the staircase. Pattie heard boots clattering on stone steps and a door bang overhead, and she was left in the firelight.

The fire was burning low. The log had fallen into grey ash so that all the illumination it gave was a faint pinkish glow. He must let it out at nights, unless he had been so mad at finding her here that he had forgotten to throw on another log.

When she got off the chair she felt stiff and slightly sick. She had had a bad shaking-up, but in retrospect perhaps that large brandy wasn't such a good idea. Nausea rose in her when she went to pick up a log and she sat back on her heels until it subsided, then placed the log carefully and slowly in the middle of the embers. Her hands were dirty and she looked at them in distaste. It would be pitch dark in the kitchen, she'd have to wait till morning, but oh, how she would love a hot bath.

Her little bathroom at home was palest blue, and she imagined herself going in there, as she did every night, slipping off her clothes and into the warm scented water. If she could do that now all the grime and the aches and pains would float away.

Her clothes felt rough against her skin. They weren't, she always wore soft pretty undies, and her sweater was cashmere. She hadn't been wearing a coat, only a jacket, when the car crashed, and she was still in her boots. Shoes might have fallen off, she was lucky she hadn't been barefoot on the mountainside, but the green tartan rug she was using as a blanket felt like barbed wire and she prickled all over.

She wished she had stayed with Michael. She clutched her charm medallion for comfort, and promised herself that as soon as dawn broke she would get up and clean herself up. But all she could do now was huddle into the chair, and watch the fire, and try to sleep again.

She couldn't remember falling asleep in front of a fire since she was a child. There were no fires in her apartment, it was all central heating, but watching the little flames flickering took her back to long-ago days when she had fallen asleep on the sofa and been safe and happy.

She shifted, trying to find an easier spot, and sighed. Any hopes of Duncan Keld agreeing to an interview had gone for sure. He wouldn't have done in any case, he still harboured a king-size grudge against her, but coming here had really cooked her goose. He couldn't have been madder. Obviously he wanted to be alone. No phone, nobody. He was probably here to work. If there was only one bed he didn't do much entertaining here, except for ladies who might share the bed. Roz and Shirley had said he was sexy, but Pattie couldn't see it. 'I'd rather be interviewed by the K.G.B.,' he'd announced—well, she'd rather sleep with Rasputin! Roll on tomorrow when she could get away, and this had to be the most uncomfortable chair she had ever encountered.

Pattie caught herself in the middle of another deep sigh of self-pity and checked it. All she had to do was remember the car at the bottom of the hill and she stopped feeling sorry for herself. Things could have been a hundred times worse.

She woke itching, with the blanket scratching her neck and face, and her hair like a bird's nest. This was disgusting, she had to get washed; and she stood up and winced, sure she was covered with bruises.

The windows were frosted over, in strange whirling patterns, so she put on another couple of logs, because her teeth were chattering, then went into the kitchen. This was a bathroom too. A second door led to a chemical loo, but you did your washing over the sink, it seemed, and Pattie's fastidiousness revolted against such primitive plumbing. Lord, it was grotty!

She tried to work the little pump over the sink and no water came. Frozen, of course. Of course it would be. Duncan Keld probably never bothered about washing. He looked a scruffy individual.

There was some water in the kettle and she poured that into a plastic bowl in the sink and soaped her hands and face. She couldn't strip. It was arctic cold in here and he could come marching in any moment. Usually she used a cream and gentle toner on her fine skin which felt tight and tender after the soaping. The towel was rough too, and she longed for the soft caressing towels at home. She had to rub to get her make-up off, but her mascara was probably streaked all over the place and—wouldn't you know it—there was no sign of a mirror.

She was trying to smooth her hair by running her fingers through it when she heard him coming and she stiffened, then stood very straight and dignified, her lips a thin disapproving line. He looked everything she disliked most in a man; appearance rough, dishevelled, his thatch of black hair unkempt and the shadow of a beard quite pronounced. Pattie shuddered when she saw him, and he shuddered too and groaned, 'Strewth, I hoped it was a nightmare!'

He was only wearing trousers. There was dark hair on his chest and arms and she felt goose-pimples on her own skin at the sight of him. He tried the pump, then picked up a big plastic jug from the corner and poured water from that over his head, standing over the sink. He seized the towel and began vigorously rubbing hair and face, at the same time looking at her as though words failed him for the moment but soon he would have a lot to say.

She said, 'Well, I'm sorry, but the interview was my editor's idea. I said you wouldn't talk to me.' She tried to defend herself. 'Although I probably did Jennifer Stanley a good turn. If the man she was going to marry was such a wet that he walked out on her because of something that happened before he met her she was well rid of him.'

'You've a point there.' He dropped the towel and looked at her straight and hard. 'But thanks to you it was probably the most publicised jilting of the year. Have you ever been rejected, Miss Ross?'

She had always played safe. She had never put herself in a situation that might end in rejection. She admitted, 'Not like that,' and he said savagely,

'Then think yourself lucky, girl.'

She did think herself lucky, every time she remembered the car. 'My car——' she began.

'Where is it?'

She explained, 'I went off the track. It's at the bottom of a hill. It's out of action, you'll have to give me a lift.'

The same expression crossed his face that she had

seen last night, when she suggested he ran her back to Grimslake. A blend of frustration and fury. He almost yelled at her, 'Damn you, I can't give you a lift! I don't have a car.'

Pattie gasped, 'But how——? I mean——'

'I come up here to work.' He sounded as though she was simple-minded and needed every word spoken very slowly. 'If I had a car I'd get in it if I got bored, so friends give me a lift here and leave me for a month.'

Marooning him, as it were. Marooning her too, God help her. She faltered, 'What if you were ill?' and he dismissed that,

'I never am.'

'There's always a first time.'

'Do you write in clichés too?' He turned away, and she shouted,

'There's nothing wrong with a good cliché if it fits!' as he slammed the door at the bottom of the stairs behind him.

If he didn't have a car and her car was out of action how was she going to get away? The enormity of her position was overwhelming her, numbing her mind. She had to get away. She couldn't stay here. Duncan Keld was back almost at once, but she had had time to start to panic and to bite hard on her lip.

She clenched her hands so that the nails bit into her palms and thought, he'll move heaven and earth to get rid of me. I won't be stuck here. He won't let it happen. She had never met a man she disliked more, but he did give an impression of power, you couldn't imagine him submitting tamely, and right now he was desperate to have his house to himself again.

He was wearing a thick black polo-necked sweater and an anorak. 'Let's go and look at this car of yours,' he said.

'Would you have a coat you could lend me?' Pattie had reached here just wearing a light jacket over her jumper and skirt, but then she had been running for her life and she had still almost been frozen. She certainly couldn't start walking in cold blood, dressed like this.

He jerked his head towards the back of the door where there was a sheepskin jacket hanging on a hook. It smothered her. It would have been funny if anything was funny today, the way the sleeves hung down, and the width of the thing. She'd be as awkward as a knight in armour in this, but the fleecy lining should keep her warm and the flapping sleeves would stop her fingers from freezing.

She said, 'So kind of you.'

He opened the door and she screamed. It was a strangled scream, but it was still a cry of horror from the heart. It couldn't have stopped snowing all night. The drift came half way up the door and out there everything was pure white, except the sky and that was still leaden grey. It wasn't snowing now, but there was more to come. She remembered the tiny flakes falling as she'd climbed in through the window and he said, 'It was thickening up when I got back.'

There was no sign of the track, nothing she recognised except the outline of the rising hills. A terrible hush and an eerie glow was over everything, and she looked at Duncan Keld and felt almost scared enough to start running the six miles to town. If she could reach the road she could hitchhike, except that nothing would come for hours, perhaps not for days.

'Well?' he said. 'Where?' and her pointing finger was shaking.

'Round there. Down.'

He strode out, through the drift that had piled against the door, on to hard frozen snow, and Pattie followed, feeling the ice down in her lungs making every breath painful. It hurt her eyes too, it was so bright and so bitter, as she kept close behind him. They couldn't see the track, but he must know it blindfold because he marched on without any hesitation and when they were roughly the distance from the house that she had covered on foot last night she began to look for her car.

She could have missed it. It was white, covered with white, in a gully that had almost filled with snow, and she called, 'There it is!' Duncan Keld looked down for what seemed to her quite a long time. Anyone else would surely have remarked on her escape, but all he did was snarl, 'Well, we can't shift it,' and glare at her as though she had done it on purpose.

The snow was starting again, large flakes this time. Looking startlingly white against his black hair, and she remembered Emily Brontë's description of Heathcliff: 'A fierce, pitiless, wolfish character.'

The wilderness all around her seemed the most dreadful place she had ever known. She must have gone crazy, only madness could have brought her here, and she looked down at her car, with her possessions in it, things she needed so badly. 'I have to get my things,' she faltered. 'I can't be without a change of clothing.' Her handbag and money and credit cards were down there, but her terror right now was not being able to wash and change her clothes. He looked at her as though she was raving and turned on his heel. She nearly called after him, but if she did he wouldn't stop, she knew that, so she began to edge her way down the hillside.

It wasn't sheer. There were hummocks and stunted bushes, all covered with snow, providing a foothold, and she went very slowly. If she could just get her small overnight case out she could clean her teeth and get herself clean, and change her undies and tights. She had her warm camel coat thrown in the back of the car, that would be a godsend, and dresses and jumpers and another skirt in the bigger case.

She was planning as she went, what she should take, how much she could carry, and then her foot slipped and she rolled, too clumsy to save herself in the enveloping sheepskin jacket, until she came up against a bush. Then she sat up, her eyes and mouth full of snow, and more snow falling, and knew she hadn't a hope of getting anything out of the car and toiling back to the top of the hill with it.

She could drown down there. If he had helped her there might have been a chance, he was so much bigger and stronger than she was. He could have pushed through the drifts at the bottom and dragged something out of the car, but she couldn't do it alone. She would have to go back, and quickly, because if the falling snow turned into a blizzard she would be lost.

Getting up was harder. She slipped several times, and she couldn't comprehend how a man could do this, leave her like this. Pitiless. Wolfish. That was right. If Roz would let her she could write such a story about him.

By the time she reached the top of the hill she was

sweating in spite of the cold from the strain and the effort. She didn't look up until she was at the top. She had climbed doggedly, head down against the falling snow, and it couldn't have taken as long as she'd thought because although Duncan Keld was walking steadily he wasn't all that far away. She scowled at his dark retreating figure and stumbled after him, and the heat she had generated died quickly so that long before she reached the lodge her face was numb with cold and her eyes were streaming.

She wouldn't put it past him to lock the doors. She wouldn't put anything past him, he was a monster. But the door opened although the frozen iron latch seemed to burn her fingers, and he was standing in front of the fire with his back towards the door and her.

He didn't look round, and Pattie let the stiff heavy coat fall to the ground and went over to the fire, as close as she dared without setting herself alight, saying 'Sorry, I'm sure you'd have preferred me to lie down and die out there, but it looks as though you're stuck with me.'

'How long before your friends come looking for you?' She shrugged, and he said sharply, 'Somebody's going to miss you, aren't they?'

'Shouldn't think so.' She moved back a little out of the blistering heat into a gentler warmth, and told him, 'Nobody knows I'm here.'

'*What?*'

'I'm supposed to be on holiday.' In a warped way she was almost enjoying this. 'But I was landed with trying to get this interview and I just thought I'd come up here.'

'Just like that?' She went on looking into the fire, and shrugged again. 'You're an impulsive idiot, aren't you?' There was no tolerance in the way he said that, only a fierce impatience. Nobody had ever called her impulsive before, but she was calling herself all kinds of idiot, and she muttered,

'I didn't know it was going to start snowing.'

'Everyone else in the county did. Don't you ever listen to weather forecasts?'

'No.' She wished now that she had turned on the radio. She wished a lot of things, all connected with being somewhere else.

'Offhand,' growled Duncan Keld, 'I can't think of anyone I'd less rather be snowed in with.'

'Snap,' she said, and she meant it every bit as much as he did.

'I'm here to work and I'm damned if you're going to stop me.' He sounded as though she would be vying for his attention, and she said contemptuously,

'I don't want to stop you. I don't want anything from you.'

'Don't get uppity with me, Miss Ross. You want my fire and my roof, but I'm very tempted to cart you as far away from here as I can and dump you.'

He looked capable of it. There was a wolfish gleam in his eyes, and Pattie sensed near-violence and said nothing. 'While you are here just sit still and shut up, and keep out of my way.' She had been kneeling in front of the fire, and he bent over her with so much menace in his face that she nodded agreeing to his terms without words. 'I work over there.' He indicated a big table some distance away. 'You can stay here.'

By the fire. That was something, being allocated a

place by the hearth. At least she wouldn't freeze to death. But she couldn't sit here mute all day long, so she ventured quite meekly, 'Could I do the cooking?'

'Leave the food alone.' He gave her a final glare of exasperation. 'Leave everything alone,' and he went off into the kitchen.

Pattie was scared to move. If she got in his way—if she went into the kitchen, for instance—he would probably shove her off her feet. He only needed the slightest excuse. He was a violent man, she remembered poor little Willie's black eye, and wondered again what had possessed her into coming up here and getting herself caged with a tiger. He was a jungle all to himself, and she found she was clutching her charm so tightly that she could feel the pull of the chain through the collar of her sweater.

'Somebody's going to miss you, aren't they?' Duncan Keld had just asked her, and nobody was. Michael might phone her apartment, but when he got no reply he would presume she was out. If she walked out of his life for ever he wouldn't miss her for long. Nobody would. She turned the charm over, tracing the happiness symbol with her forefinger, and wondered if she had ever been happy. I miss you, she thought. In all these years I've never stopped missing you.

Duncan Keld came out of the kitchen with a tray holding a mug, a flask, and a plateful of sandwiches, and without a glance at Pattie settled himself at the big table. She watched him, she had nothing else to do, as he took papers out of drawers and a file and a typewriter from another chair.

She envied him, with all the equipment for his work. She would have liked a few sheets of paper and the loan of a ballpoint. She could have written some letters if nothing else. As soon as he seemed immersed in what he was doing, which was almost at once, she got up very quietly and tiptoed as softly as she could in boots into the kitchen.

There were three cupboards in here, and she opened the tall narrow one. It was like opening a mummy case, seeing the long tin bath standing up inside. Pattie could imagine that in front of a roaring fire. You would have to heat the water to fill it and then empty it again, but if she could be sure of privacy she would be tempted to try it. Duncan Keld could hardly have a bath while she was here, unless he sent her upstairs, and to her mental pictures of the steaming bath was added the figure of a man, dark and stark and pouring water over himself as he had done over his head in the kitchen this morning. He'd be hairy all over, she decided with a shudder, revoltingly hirsute; and she shut the door sharply, shutting off that image.

Another small cupboard had first aid ointments and lotions and a bottle of aspirins. He might never be ill, that's what he'd said, but this would be useful in minor mishaps, and if she couldn't sleep tonight she would take a couple of aspirins.

The third cupboard was the food cupboard, and well stocked with tins and packages, eggs, bacon and several loaves of brown bread. Most of it convenience food, but he wouldn't go hungry if he stayed his month out, and he could have let her prepare the meals. She could have goulashed the corned beef and pepped up the soups. She wasn't hungry. On the contrary, she felt an aversion to food that made her queasy at the sight of it, even tinned. She took one plain water biscuit and nibbled a little, but her mouth tasted sour because she hadn't been able to clean her teeth.

But a cup of tea or coffee would be different, and there was still hot water in the kettle. If Duncan Keld had just used the stove it had to be safe, so she lit one of the burners and boiled up the water and found a tea bag, then made tea in a blue enamel mug adding sugar and powdered milk.

There wasn't much to see through the narrow little window through which she had made her entry yesterday. The snow was like a white lace curtain across it, only you couldn't draw this curtain. She had been glad enough to get in yesterday, that fire had saved her life. He must have been here earlier to light the fire. Someone must have taken him away and brought him back again and when they brought him back said, 'Goodbye, see you in four weeks' time.'

If she had been awake instead of sleeping the sleep of exhaustion and brandy she could have hitched a lift, but now she was stuck until the snow went away, or somebody found her car and started looking for her. They'd come here first. This was the nearest house, the only house for miles.

'Somebody come looking for me,' she prayed, and remembered standing at other windows whispering a similar prayer, 'Please come. You told me to wait and be good. Oh, please come back!'

She was getting lightheaded. She had to keep her head because that was a brutal man in there. If she broke down she'd get no pity from him. She took what was left of the hot tea back to the fire—it was freezing in the kitchen—and drank it to the dregs. Then she picked up the sheepskin coat she had worn from the floor, just inside the front door, where she'd dropped it.

The snow had melted on it, making a small pool on the flagstones, and she had been a fool not to shake it before she dumped it, she could be wanting it again. She draped it over a chair, and put another log on the fire.

Duncan Keld had told her to leave the food alone. She didn't want his food, but the fire was another matter. If he stopped her building up the fire she would go berserk. There were all those logs outside so he would have no excuse, and she sat on the goat-skin rug with her back to the easy chair, watching the sparks go up the chimney.

After a while her head began to nod. She pushed a cushion up against the chair arm, rested her head on it and closed her eyes and dozed. She was tired. The trek out to the car had been strenuous, and the warmth of the fire and the rhythm of a tapping type-writer lulled her. She didn't know how long she slept, but when she opened her eyes she heard this deep slow sexy voice.

She knew at once where she was. Her heart sank and she closed her eyes again. He wasn't talking to her. He was speaking on a tape recorder, describing something mechanical. Something to do with a boat maybe, and she lay still and listened. She decided that when he wasn't growling or snarling, he had an attractive voice. Some women might describe it as sexy and wonder how it would sound if he said something very personal and intimate, and just for them.

Pattie shocked herself rigid with that thought and jerked herself upright. There wasn't even a book

about that she could see. Maybe there was in cupboards or drawers, but how would Duncan Keld
react if she started wandering around, poking into
corners?

He had turned off the tape recorder now and he
was typing again, and she coughed and said, 'Excuse
me.'

No reply, no sign that he had heard her, so she
asked, 'Are you actually blocking me out or just pretending to?' Still he didn't seem to hear, although of
course he knew she was speaking to him, and she
began to get extremely irritated. He was such a lout,
so uncouth. 'Oh, the concentration of the man!' she
shrilled with phoney enthusiasm. 'I think it's wonderful! Oh, I envy you that. I've been sitting here
and trying to think myself somewhere else, but I
can't. I have this lovely picture in my head of being
somewhere I can clean my teeth, like back home,
but all the time I know I'm here.'

He turned in his chair then, gave her a look of flat
dislike and said, 'One more word and you're out.'

'It does hear,' she mocked. 'Just testing.' But as he
got to his feet she added hastily, 'I'll be quiet,' because although she was sure he wouldn't carry out
his threat she was surprised how relieved she felt
when he sat down again.

Her bruises were aching. They had been all day.
She had tender patches all over, particularly where
the safety-belt had held her, saving her from worse.
But now she seemed to be aching more than ever,
and she remembered the lotion for sprains in the first
aid cupboard in the kitchen and wondered if that
would help.

With nothing else to do except sit here she could

feel each throbbing spot, and she would have to help herself because nobody else was going to. She wished she could have stayed by the fire to administer the treatment, but she would have as soon stripped off in the middle of Piccadilly Circus as in front of Duncan Keld, even if he was blocking her out.

She nearly changed her mind when she stood in the cold kitchen, and as she peeled off her sweater she felt her skin turn clammy. She slithered out of the straps of her slip and wriggled that down to her waist, then started checking and was surprised that she didn't look worse. Perhaps the bruises hadn't come out yet. She felt that she ought to be black and blue, but perhaps her solarium suntan was masking the damage.

She wrinkled her nose at the pungent smell of the lotion. If it got on her clothes she had no chance of washing them, and she couldn't bear anything soiled near her skin. Her general feeling of grubbiness was already becoming a phobia with her, and she unhooked her bra and dropped it on the table, then very gingerly began to dab her rib-cage where it hurt.

She screamed, 'Get out!' as the door opened, and the lotion went spinning as she flung her arms convulsively across her breasts, but she could have been fully dressed for all the effect it had on him.

'If you get pneumonia,' he said, 'don't expect me to nurse you,' and he went to the cupboard and took out a packet of biscuits, then walked out without giving her a second look.

By this time she was scrabbling back into her slip, and even after the door was closed she went on dressing as fast as though he was in here staring at her.

Everything stank of the lotion. The bottle was broken and acrid fumes were filling the room. She shouldn't have panicked like that. Duncan Keld must have seen many a topless girl in his life, both privately and publicly, and her figure was good. She had firm pretty breasts and the last thing in the world she wanted was to turn him on, but it was a sort of insult that he hadn't turned a hair.

She finished dressing, pulling her jumper well down over her hips, and buttoning her jacket, then she set about cleaning up the mess, sweeping the glass splinters with a broom on to a shovel and tipping them into a plastic bin that stood by the door. She got a bowl of snow to swab the floor, and another bowl to wash her hands, and by then her fingers were blue and completely without feeling. When she got back to the fire they throbbed almost unbearably for what seemed like ages. A lot of good all that had done for her health, and she sat staring broodingly into the flames.

Darkness crept into the room almost unnoticed so far as Pattie was concerned. She realised that the shadows were thickening at her back when Duncan Keld got up and lit the lamp. But he kept it on the table where he was working, so she only got a fringe benefit, although the diffused glow could have been quite pleasant, in other circumstances and other company.

The house, Wuthering Heights, must have been rather like this lodge. Perhaps she could write an article about that, about being snowed in with Heathcliff. She could remember the story, of course, it had been one of her favourite books when she was young, and she looked across at the man sitting in

the lamplight, and phrases ran through her mind . . .
'The cheeks were sallow and half covered in black
whiskers' . . . He hadn't shaved today, he probably
didn't while he was up here on his own and he wasn't
going to bother for her. Another day or two and they
would look like a couple of tramps. More than another two days, she thought, and I shall go crazy
. . . 'The eyes deep set and singular.' He looked up,
turned his head slightly, saw her eyes on him and
scowled. 'A half-civilised ferocity' . . . Pattie recalled,
and smiled at the aptness of that, amused by the
little game she was playing, when he said, 'I hope
you're not writing this article of yours in your head.'

She gasped, because it was as though he had read
her mind, flushing scarlet and hoping the light was
dim enough to hide it as he got up and came towards
her. She scrambled to her feet, she wasn't crouching
down here at *his* feet, and he said, 'What kind of
questions would you be asking?'

He wasn't co-operating, she was sure of that. They
stood, facing each other, and his nearness was so
oppressive that she could hardly breathe. 'What do
you know about me?' he asked. Pattie could hardly
speak. She knew that everything about him seemed a
threat. She knew all the facts she had read in his
envelope in the office library. She said jerkily, 'What
other people have written.'

'Bad,' he shook his head reprovingly at her. The
beard shadow was heavy. Michael had such a smooth
skin, she had never seen him even remotely in need
of a shave. The sheer animal maleness of this man
horrified her, and then he said, 'You need personal
experience,' and she did stop breathing, because he
was looking at her, at her face, at her body, as though

he was assessing her. And for *what*?

'You're no beauty, Pattie Ross,' he said at last, 'but you're a woman and you're here. Don't you think that your readers would prefer it if you could say I made a pass at you?'

Her breath came out choking, 'Don't be ridiculous!'

'Oh, I'm not.' He was smiling, but that didn't reassure her at all. 'Not as a lover, I assure you. What else do you suggest we do to pass the time?'

He put hands on her shoulders. The touch was light but she felt as though he was gripping her and she shuddered and, croaked, 'Let me go!'

'I wish I could.' Although he wasn't holding her any longer she could still feel his hands. 'But that's the trouble, you won't go.'

She couldn't go, there was no way, and for a moment she believed she was about to be ravished and she knew she would go mad, then he laughed and said, 'You wouldn't be worth the fuss.'

He was baiting her, deliberately terrifying her. She said shakily, 'I hate you,' and he said,

'I'm not too crazy about you—and I'll tell you something else, you're sure as hell not growing on me.'

He ate in silence, a meal of cold ham and pickles, bread and cheese which he brought from the kitchen and ate at his work table. There was no suggestion that Pattie should eat, and she couldn't have swallowed anything. She just sat by the fire, waiting to be left alone, willing him to go upstairs, but when he did he took the lamp with him. There was another one hanging from a beam, but she didn't know how to use it, so when he went she was in darkness, except for the firelight.

It was still snowing outside. She opened the back door and looked into a whirling whiteness and sobbed, almost silently, although Duncan Keld couldn't have heard her, not from upstairs he couldn't. It was years since she had felt so vulnerable and so helpless. Never in her life had she met a man who showed her such contempt and such antagonism. Today had lessened none of it, and if things went on like this there would be an explosion, because whenever he looked at her violence never seemed far beneath the surface.

She built up the fire, so high that the room was quite bright with it. At least she was warm and she might get to sleep. She would probably have nightmares, but as she tried to settle herself in the lumpy old chair she wondered why she should worry about bad dreams when she was already trapped in this waking nightmare.

CHAPTER THREE

PATTIE had a restless night. Her aches and pains and the stress of her situation would have made it hard for her to sleep peacefully in the most luxurious of beds, but stuck in an old armchair it was a wonder she slept at all. And there was nothing better. A large sofa stood at the other end of the room, long enough to stretch out on, but Victorian horsehair, which meant it was as hard as a board and weighed a ton. Pattie didn't think she could drag it to the fire.

She had to be by the fire, and she was sure that if she tried Duncan Keld would hear her and might come down to see what she was doing.

She dreaded that. She didn't expect to see him again before morning, but she knew that if there was any sound of movement in the rooms above, much less of footsteps on the stairs, she would be scared out of her wits.

He didn't fancy her. She wasn't his type. The state she was in now she couldn't see how she could be anybody's type, but as he'd said, she was a woman and she was here, and suppose he got drunk. There were several bottles down here on the Welsh dresser in the kitchen. There might be more upstairs, and he looked the sort who might get drunk. Pattie did have nightmares. They were wild and violent, and she woke from them with every sense alert, straining to hear and staring into the shadows.

As soon as it began to get light she went into the kitchen, scooped up snow from the drift that had blown against the door in the night and heated it in the kettle. She was listening all the while. She could only guess at the time, somewhere between six and seven, she thought, because her watch was in her jewel case in the car. She didn't wear a wrist-watch, she had a slim gold modern fob-watch that hung on a chain round her neck. The chain belonged to her amulet. She had been wearing that, and she was so glad she had because she couldn't have left that behind. Somehow or other she would have dug down for that.

There were still two wrapped loaves, and a half loaf, and after she had washed she spread herself a slice of bread and butter which she had to force down. She didn't know whether it was because it was Duncan Keld's food that made everything so unappetising, she wanted *nothing* of his, or because she had just lost all appetite. She might have picked at a dish that was cooked and served daintily, as a convalescent would, but scraping rock-hard butter, and trying to make it adhere to three days old bread turned her stomach. She couldn't face cheese or bacon, she couldn't really face anything, but she did boil the kettle and make tea and take a mug of that back to the fire.

Before he got down she looked around for something to read today, and wished she had the courage to help herself to pen and paper. The paper on the table was covered with writing or typing, but there would surely be a supply in the drawers, and what was a sheet or two of paper? It was enough to spark off a row, that's what it was. He was just looking for excuses to insult her, and if she opened the drawers of his work-table she would be asking for it.

But she did find some old National Geographic magazines and took those to her spot by the fireplace, then she heard him coming downstairs and sat, arms folded and fingers gripping. He walked through the room as though it was empty and Pattie thought, that's what I've got to do, I've got to block him out the way he does me, and tell myself he isn't there.

Only it was impossible. She didn't have to look, but she couldn't close her ears. She leafed through a magazine, but she could hear him clattering around in the kitchen, and smell bacon frying. That made her queasier than ever. She was glad he stayed where he was to eat it, but she was still following his movements, and when the door opened and he came back into the room she couldn't help turning.

Of course he hadn't shaved. He looked like a hairy ape, and her face clenched and he said, 'You look pretty rough yourself,' and Pattie thought, not as rough as I feel. Tonight after he's gone upstairs I'll wash my underclothes and dry them in front of the fire. She said nothing, and the sound of his typewriter soon filled the silence.

She didn't mind that. It was a familiar sound, she had always worked among clattering typewriters. The wind was rising. She could hear it howling in the great chimney, and she read her magazines very slowly, not missing a word, trying to put herself into the pictures.

When she was a child she had expected to travel all over the world. Her father was an overseas radar expert for an international engineering firm, although most of his trips were brief he was sometimes away for months on end, and when Pattie was through with school he had promised to take her along. She had always wanted to write. She had sold short stories to children's magazines when she was quite young, monopolised the school magazine and got glowing reports from her English teacher. She was going to travel with her father, meet people, write real books, but it hadn't happened.

She couldn't complain about her life. She had been lucky to get the breaks she had had, but it could have been different, she could have been different. She had never been afraid of anything while her father was alive, and look at her now, hardly daring to breathe for fear of the man at the other end of the room. Of course he wouldn't touch her. He was no fool, he would know what the consequences would be and as he had pointed out, she wasn't worth the fuss. He wouldn't harm her. Not physically. Mentally she could harm herself, and perhaps she *was* heading for a breakdown.

She hadn't been herself for some time, and now she had nothing to do but sit and think she faced the fact. She longed for Michael now, and the soft easy life he represented, but before she came here she had sensed something missing in their relationship. She had been restless, she had wanted to break out in some way, but she surely hadn't bargained for what she'd got. It had been like taking a stroll on your own down a country lane, and ending up in a jungle.

By the roaring log fire it was as hot as a jungle, but out there was a frozen world. She had to keep the log supply high and dry, so she put on the sheepskin coat and went out through the back door. The flakes were still drifting down, not heavily, but that was no guarantee that the worst was over. The colour of the sky hadn't lightened much. The way the snow stopped, then started again, was enough to snap your nerves. Like opening a prison door by a tiny crack and banging it shut.

I'm full of little fancies, Pattie thought. Next thing I'll be mumbling them aloud to myself for company, and when he says, 'I told you to be quiet,' I'll say, 'Who, me? I never said a word,' and I'll believe it.

The log pile was buried under deep snow, but there was a shovel in the kitchen, and she scraped and dug down to the soaking wet wood. She would have given a lot to have been wearing gloves when the car crashed. Even thin leather ones would have been a godsend. Her hands were frozen, and she carried in the logs three at a time—which was as many as she could manage—and stacked them neatly, a safe but drying distance from the fire.

Duncan Keld never looked at her. He was in his own little world and although she was going about her task as quietly as possible she still resented his concentration. If she wondered off into the snowy wastes he wouldn't notice she'd gone until night fell and he lit the lamp. He wouldn't go looking for her then. The ego of the man! All he thought about was himself. The way her getting stuck here had inconvenienced him. Well, it was no birthday party for her.

At least anger was warming. When she decided she had enough logs indoors to last for a while she walked around outside at the back of the house, her hands tucked into her sleeves. The wind was blowing the top snow in spiralling flurries, and several times the frozen surface gave way and she was up to her knees in softer snow.

She stayed close to the house. She had never taken a good look at the back before. There were four windows up there, which must surely mean more than one bedroom, and although Duncan Keld said there was only one bed there might be a camp-bed, or even sheets. It would be lovely to wrap herself up in a sheet instead of that hairy smelly travelling rug.

The door at the bottom of the stairs creaked slightly, but the typewriter probably drowned that, and the sound of her footsteps on the stone steps. Two doors led from the little landing at the top of the stairs. Pattie opened one and closed it very quickly because it was obviously Duncan Keld's bedroom and she had no desire to go poking around in there. She gave a little grimace which she couldn't have explained, because the glance had shown it to be fairly tidy with white sheets on a turned down bed.

The second room was big, at least twice the size of the first, very cold, and empty except for a couple of old trunks. The walls were white and the roof beams were black and in summer it would have been pleasant with windows both sides letting in the light, but it didn't look as if it was in use summer or winter. There wasn't even a rug on the bare boards of the floor.

Pattie breathed on one of the windows to melt a peephole, rubbing the frost away and looking out over the unbroken white landscape. It was the most desolate scene she had ever seen, like a dead planet, and she thought how wonderful it would be to spy a snowplough in the distance, or helicopter in the sky— although could helicopters land on snow? There wasn't a helicopter. There wasn't even a bird. And she would have to go down to the fire because she was shivering again.

She got through that day thanks to the magazines. There were actually times when the articles and pictures transported her for a little while, and time passed, and when the light started to fade she read by the firelight, moving closer to the flames.

She saw Duncan Keld lighting the lamp, then he went into the kitchen and she thought, that's another day nearly through, now for the night, only the nights are worse, and automatically she went to hold her amulet. But it had gone. She was no longer wearing it, and she fumbled frantically round her throat as though the chain might have slipped inside the high neck of her sweater. Then she jumped to her feet and pulled off her jacket, but it wasn't there, and she stared around on the chair and on the rug and in the circle of firelight where she had spent most of the day, her head jerking from side to side, her eyes wild.

Her sense of loss was enormous. She would have been heartbroken at losing it any time, but here, where she was so miserable and under such strain, it tipped the balance of her self-control into hysteria so that she hardly knew what she was doing.

But she had to find it again, she knew that, and she had been upstairs. So she ran up the stairs, into the big empty room where through the failing light she could see nothing on the floor but the faint mark of her own footsteps in the dust.

Oh God, she thought, outside! I went to the woodpile how many times? I walked around. I could have dropped it in the snow. The chain was so fragile, I must have weakened a link. Last night I nearly jerked it off.

It had been snowing again since she brought in the wood. It would be covered and it was getting dark: she would have to wait till morning, although it could still be in the house. She had been in the kitchen, to the loo, earlier she had walked around looking for something to read, opening a cupboard and finding the magazines. She was by the cupboard, peering in corners, when he came back into the room and said, 'Will you stop prowling around like a caged cat?'

She said jerkily, 'I've lost my charm.'

'What?'

'My good luck charm. It's Chinese. My father gave it to me.' It wasn't here. He had left the lamp on the table, it threw shadows, but she would have seen the moon-pale glimmer of white onyx.

'Well, ask Daddy to buy you another,' he drawled.

'I can't. He can't.' The muscles in her jaws tightened. After all these years she could still hardly bring herself to say it. 'He's—dead.'

'I'm sorry,' he said, and she spat at him,

'No, you're not. Why should you be? It's nothing to do with you.'

'When?'

'A long time ago. Years.' She went to hold the charm again and her fingers closed on nothing, and she felt the tears burning her eyes and choked, 'I've kept it for years and now I've lost it, up here, maybe in the snow where I'll never find it, and you stand there saying you're sorry. You *hypocrite*!' Disgust and rage rose in her, pounding in her temples so that she thought her head would burst. She would have killed him if she could. It was an insensate fury, mindless as a child's or a madwoman's, that could only be appeased by violence. 'To hell with you!' she screamed, 'and your beastly rotten stupid work!'

It was sheer luck she didn't sweep the lamp off the table. She swept papers away, she would have liked to tear them to pieces. She wanted to hurl the typewriter against the wall because it was a symbol of him being all right, busy, well fed, while she was in pieces because she had just lost the last thing her father ever gave her.

But he reached her before she could lift it, and she shrieked at him that if somebody didn't get her out of here right *now* she would go crazy. She couldn't breathe and she couldn't bear it any longer, and keep away from her and don't touch her, or she would claw his eyes out.

He hit her across the face, and she was so hysterical that at first she hardly felt the pain. Something jerked her head back and cut off the babble of words, then she felt her cheek smarting and lifted a hand to cover it, and heard herself whisper, 'Now you've blacked my eye. Just like Willie's.'

'No,' he said, 'not like Willie's.'

It was like a douch of cold water. Pattie gasped and choked and shook her head as though she was being held under a shower, then the hot anger drained away, her skin turned cold and she began to shiver uncontrollably.

She had never before made such a spectacle of herself. As a child she had had tantrums, what child doesn't, but never like this and never since she was a child. She had been proud of her self-control, but just now she had been like somebody possessed; and she was still acting out of character because now she couldn't stop crying and it was years since she had wept.

She hiccuped, 'Excuse me', and thought how ridiculous that sounded. Her head was still throbbing, the tears were still flowing, and the only handkerchief she had was in her jacket pocket over there by the fire. She could hardly see her way for tears. She gulped and said, 'That's the first time I was ever hysterical. I do—apologise.'

Duncan Keld put a handkerchief into her hand that was soft and smelt clean and fresh and she said, 'Oh, thank you,' and buried her face in it. 'I'm so sorry,' she mumbled through the folds of cambric. 'I don't ever cry and now I can't stop.'

'You will,' he said. 'The crying always stops.'

This was when she would have expected him to rage at her or cut her down with bitter taunts, but his voice was gentle and when she looked at him he drew her to him and held her, and it was inexpressibly comforting.

She had never wept in any man's arms but her father's, and that had only been for childish things. She felt weak as a child now. She stumbled as he led her back to the fire, and she curled up in the huge lumpy armchair, which was big enough for two because he sat down in it too, and she was curled up against him, with his arms around her.

'It was the last thing he gave me,' she sobbed, 'before he went away for the last time. He said when he came back he wanted to see me wearing it, and I think I used to believe that as long as I wore it he might come back.'

'We'll find it,' he promised. 'If you dropped it in here we'll find it tomorrow.'

'It could be outside.'

'Then that will take a little longer.' The beard was dark now, but she thought, it's quite a face. Not handsome. Not smooth, regular features like Michael's. But rugged and strong and in a way beautiful.

'I'll pick your papers up in a minute,' she said. 'I don't know what happened to me. My mind seemed to snap when I saw I'd lost my charm. Perhaps it's because I haven't been eating.'

'You *what*?' The dark brows came together.

'You told me to leave the food alone.'

He stared at her. 'And you *did*?'

'I wasn't hungry.'

'Wait a minute, let me get this straight.' He sounded incredulous. 'You've not been eating for the last two days? Are you anorexic?'

'No. You said leave it alone.'

'Sure I did. I said leave everything alone. I said sit down there and don't make a move. But I didn't expect you to do it, you stupid woman.'

Of course it was stupid. She said, 'I know, I know. It was stupid coming here. It was stupid running my car off the road. I was nearly killed and I was scared to death and I thought I'd rather starve than touch your food. I've felt sick ever since I got here, I haven't *wanted* any food. I still don't. I just want to find my amulet.'

Duncan Keld said, 'Tomorrow we find the amulet. Tonight we eat.' He stood up. 'Stay right where you are.'

Pattie wasn't hungry, but when he brought two bowls of soup she swallowed a little and soon found herself scraping the bottom of the bowl. Duncan was watching her as he drank his soup. She had the big chair to herself now, he was seated in a wooden arm-chair. 'Better?' he asked.

'Yes, thank you. May I put on another log?'

He placed two logs on the embers, and she heard herself say, 'Would you come and sit here, please?' because she needed somebody to be close to her. She said, 'If you would just hold me,' and when he did she tensed for a moment, then relaxed and said, 'I'm sorry I barged in on you.'

He grinned. Pattie had never seen him smile like this before. When the smile reached his eyes she had to smile back. 'I wasn't planning on company,' he explained. 'I'm a psycho-case about being alone every so often,' and then, changing the subject, 'Tell me about your father,' and she knew it was what she wanted to do.

That was strange, because she never talked about her past. Her friends knew that her only relative was her mother, they knew her background, but she started to tell Duncan Keld what kind of man her father had been, how kind and clever and funny. She told him about life in the old house, things that she thought she had forgotten: the way her bedroom looked out over the apple orchard, the names of old friends and neighbours, the great tree that stood in the entrance hall each Christmas and how her father always managed to get home for Christmas. 'More than once he arrived on Christmas Eve and sometimes he had to go away again early in the new year, but he always came, we always knew he would.'

He was flying home on Christmas Eve when his plane hit a mountainside. Pattie had heard the news flash when she was alone in the house. Her mother had been at a carol service, Pattie had stayed behind because they only knew her father was coming, they had no definite time, and she had stayed home to welcome him.

'I knew as soon as I heard them say it that it was his flight.' She sounded very young and very sad. 'They give you a number you can ring and I kept trying to ring it and I couldn't get through, and then my mother came home with a crowd of friends, and they were laughing and joking and it was ages before I could get one of them to listen to me.'

'How old were you?'

'Fifteen.' Her face was smudged, a pointed elfin face, with hair falling lankly, and Duncan lifted a strand and tucked it gently behind her ear. 'I never cried. Not at all.' She sounded as though that still surprised her. 'I suppose it was because my mother broke down and I had her to look after and I daren't let go. And maybe I didn't believe it.'

His hand warmed her, around her shoulder, and she felt as though she could fall asleep and there would be no nightmares. 'I always missed him,' she said. 'When he gave me the charm he said, "When you wear this I'll know and I'll be thinking of you," and I used to pretend he still could. I used to tell myself that one day when I was wearing it he would come back. I will find it again, won't I?'

'Of course you will.'

She had never been cuddled since her father died. It took her back over the years, and her lids drooped heavily. She was very tired, but when Duncan said, 'Come to bed,' she bit her lip and started to stammer, 'No, I——'

'I know what you need,' he said.

He might be right, she didn't want to be alone again tonight. But he looked down at her with an expression that only held kindness and said, 'Sleep and warmth,' then he picked her up and carried her as easily as if she was still a child. She linked her hands around his neck and her head dropped against him, and when he put her in the bed the sheets were cold for a moment, but he lay down beside her, still dressed, still holding her.

It was her first untroubled sleep in this house, and it was deep and dreamless. She half woke once, and wriggled out of her skirt and jumper. She knew Duncan was there. Or rather she knew that some-body was with her with whom she was safe, and she yawned and snuggled down and slipped back into slumber . . .

The next time she woke it was morning. The bed was empty, she was alone, and she lay there, her mind clear, feeling as though she had come out of a dark tunnel into the light. She thought wryly, a psychiatrist would have charged me a fortune to have released all those inhibitions; because last night she had done her weeping for her father's death. Tears that had been held back for years had been shed.

There was an indentation in the pillow where Duncan's head had rested and she sat up, knees hunched, looking at it. 'Thank you, doctor,' she said. 'I'm glad to have met you. You did me a power of good last night. You're a super man.'

'Tea or coffee?' he called from the bottom of the stairs.

'Either,' she called back. 'Whatever's least trouble,' and her voice seemed to have a singing note.

'They're both hot water poured on a bag.'

'Coffee, then, please.'

You couldn't tell if it was still snowing, the windows were still white, but today she must search outside for her amulet, and if she didn't find it right away—well, nobody else was going to. It would wait for her, wherever it was.

When she heard him coming up the stairs her heart gave a funny little jump and she watched the open doorway half smiling, her heart beating fast. Duncan was dressed, she couldn't remember if he had been dressed all night, but his face looked damp and clean and she said, 'You shaved. Oh, *lovely*!'

He grinned, 'Yes, I am, aren't I?'

She felt warm and happy and crazy. 'It's an improvement all right, but I wasn't talking about you. What I meant was it has to mean there's a mirror around here some place. I could do with a mirror.' She pulled a lock of her hair and squinted sidewards at it. It looked like seaweed. And her hands and her face were grubby and she was a mess.

'You look all right,' he said, and gave her the mug of hot coffee.

'You're lying.' But Pattie no longer felt degraded by her scruffiness. She could laugh about it, and he shook his head, 'No, I'm not,' and she knew that he thought she was pretty.

He went to a chest of drawers and opened one, and she sipped her coffee and watched. He was tall, broad-shouldered. His black hair curled slightly over the polo-neck of his sweater and she had a sudden urge to get out of bed and go across and stand behind him and put her hands over his eyes and say, 'Guess who?' because she wanted to touch him. Like she had touched the amulet, for luck and security? But she smiled wryly at that idea, because it was not at all the same. She said, 'I'm sorry about last night, making such a fool of myself.'

'You didn't.'

Anyone else would have thought she had. She went on, 'And for landing myself on you.'

Duncan turned from the chest of drawers, putting a brown and white checked shirt on top. 'That,' he said, 'was a shaker.'

'You could put it stronger.'

'That I could.' They both laughed and he went on, 'It was pretty galling being observed by a journalist who'd come to write about me, and every time

I looked up there you were, brooding in the chimney piece, looking downright malevolent.'

She grimaced, 'I thought you were horrible.'

'I am,' he agreed cheerfully. 'I'm so bloody horrible that I'm not fit to be let loose full time among my fellow human beings, especially when a book gets to the nitty-gritty. That's when I come up here and shut myself in and hope for something to keep the rest of them out. Like snow. But I'm not often this lucky with the weather.'

He was a man who had to be alone, she could understand that. No man is an island, the poet said, but Duncan was pretty nearly one. Pattie sat with her chin on her knees, hands clasped around her ankles, surveying him with wide dark eyes. 'This makes it like a little island, doesn't it?' she said. 'Only you've got a castaway. Or a stowaway. Are you going to throw me out?'

He had threatened to. He might have done, but she was safe now. 'There were moments,' he said. But when she cracked and tried to destroy his work and ran wild he had shown only compassion. She promised, 'I'll be as quiet as a mouse,' and wrinkled her nose, twitching mouselike, and he laughed,

'Come on down and I'll show you where I keep the cheese.'

She was wearing a slip, bra, pants and tights, but when she threw back the bedclothes and stepped out she suddenly felt absurdly shy. Her nervous little laugh must have sounded as though the cold air had hit her, because he said, 'Get dressed by the fire.'

'Yes,' she said, 'all right, and please would you have anything you could lend me while I wash my undies, like a shirt?'

'Take your pick.' He nodded towards the chest of drawers. 'I'll see about breakfast and you'd better be hungry.'

She giggled again. She was feeling nervous as a kitten; and excited, because everything had changed. The lodge was no longer her prison, more like a spaceship heading for the stars.

Pattie took two shirts. There were plenty of them, so she picked out two, one for days and one for nights, because she could well be here another week or so. She got into the day shirt, cinched it in at the waist with her belt, then threw back the bedclothes and started to make the bed.

There was a double sleeping bag, with sheets and pillows and a duvet thrown over, and a good springy mattress. She made it neatly and stood back and looked down at it, and found she was blushing and knew that there was a glow about her.

Her boots clattered on the stairs as she hurried down. She didn't need to creep any more. She would be unobtrusive while Duncan was working, of course, but he had forgiven her for being here—and what was more she had forgiven herself. So now she would make the best of it. She would get her article and she might get a very good friend. She might get just about the best friend she had ever had.

He was in the kitchen, at the stove, and again her heart gave that little leap at the sight of him. She asked, 'Are you good at the cooking as well?'

'Cordon Bleu it's not,' he said. 'But my scrambled eggs aren't to be sneezed at.'

'I don't——' she began, and he turned from the stove and pointed a fork at her.

'If you're going to say you don't like scrambled

eggs you get what you do eat, because I don't want you flaking out from starvation.'

'Honestly,' she protested, 'I eat most things, and I like scrambled eggs. What I was going to say was, "I don't suppose you'd let me cook dinner?"'

'Splendid idea!' He sounded all for it, and that would pass the day for her.

'What time?' she asked.

'Sevenish.'

'Just one hitch, I don't have a watch. It's in my handbag in my car.'

Duncan took off the heavy Cartier wristwatch he wore and put it on the kitchen table. 'And now,' he said, 'you can make the toast.'

There was a long brass toasting fork with slightly bent prongs, and Pattie held the bread close to the embers and watched it curling and browning, and thought how much more satisfying this was than popping slices into a metallic container and waiting for them to be hurled back at you.

They ate breakfast in front of the fire. The toast had a faintly smoky taste, but Pattie still preferred it to the kind she had at home, and Duncan was right about the scrambled eggs, they were good. She ate hungrily, and so did he, as though he was in a hurry to finish and start work. She would have liked to talk, but the talking could wait. She had a feeling of timelessness. There was no urgency about today. Later they would talk, and it wasn't just for her article that she wanted to know about him.

He finished before her and took his plate and mug into the kitchen, while Pattie chewed on the final crust of her toast and debated with herself about making another slice. The bread would be too stale to eat soon, and only get wasted, and she was giving the matter her serious consideration, sitting in the fireglow, when he handed her an oblong mirror in a narrow white plastic frame. 'Sure you want this?' he asked.

Her reflection made her wince and she wailed, 'I'm sorry I asked for it now. Talk about the raggle-taggle gipsies! Could I have a borrow of your comb? You do have a comb?'

'Look, lady,' he glared at her, but it was mock pugnacity that made her laugh, 'on my own up here I grow a beard—a handsome one too, basically I'm a hairy feller—but my general habits are hygienic. I comb my hair, I clean my teeth, I wash—all over.'

She grinned. 'Oh, what's wrong with a bit of scruffiness?' and couldn't believe what she was saying. 'But I would like to wash my hair.'

'Hang on,' he said. This time he went upstairs, and came back at once, carrying a bottle of amber-coloured liquid. 'I hadn't unpacked this.' Pattie gave a delighted squeal. 'Never got so much appreciation for so little before,' he said.

'Who wants perfume, chocolates, red roses?' she chortled theatrically. 'This is *beautiful*!' She kissed the bottle of shampoo and Duncan said,

'Now that's a waste of a good kiss. I gave it to you.'

He stooped and kissed her lips and the light touch of his mouth sent ice-cold pins and needles up and down her spine.

'But right now,' he said, 'work.'

'Of course,' she said.

Work for him, but she was going to wash her hair and make herself presentable. If she could achieve that she would work on the next stage and try to end up looking seductive. She had longed for her luggage ever since she arrived here, but now more than ever she sighed for a change into pretty clothes, and something to brighten her lips and cheeks. She was naturally pale. The golden tan she acquired through her weekly sessions under the sun-lamps needed to be augmented with a cheek blusher and lipstick, but here she had neither.

A few months ago she had written an article on the ways Victorian ladies cheated before cosmetics became respectable. Beetroot was one aid. It stained red, and if you applied it lightly and quickly it didn't look too hectic. There was a jar of pickled beetroot in the kitchen cupboard and she wondered about trying that out for lipstick and if it would leave her smelling and tasting of vinegar, and burst into giggles, and Duncan, who was sorting out papers at his work table, asked, 'What's the joke?'

'Er—do you like vinegar?' He probably thought she was thinking about dinner, but he'd wonder why that should strike her as funny. 'Just a taste,' she added.

'Sure.' He waited for further explanation and getting none went on with his paper sorting. He had picked up the work she had strewn around last night, before she came down this morning. She should have done that. She wouldn't have known what order to put it in, but she could have gathered it up from the floor and apologised again. She said, 'I'm—sorry about that.'

'What?' This time he wasn't quite on her wavelength. It took him a moment to realise she was speaking, another to understand what she was talking about. 'Forget it,' he said, and Pattie knew she must shut up now.

She thought, thank God I didn't get the chance to burn any papers, that I didn't manage to lift the typewriter and smash it. She had done no real damage. She wondered how Duncan would have reacted if she had, because although he had been understanding he was not a tolerant man. If she had snarled up his work he might have hit her for real.

Lucky for me, she thought, and although she was without her health-and-happiness charm she had never felt so lucky in her life. Of course she desperately wanted to find it, but when she opened the back door fresh snow had covered her footsteps and her diggings into the wood pile. She would find nothing out there today, especially as tiny flakes were still falling.

She found herself smiling at them, and knew she would have been disappointed if there had been signs of a thaw. She no longer wanted to get away. Some time fairly soon, of course, but not until she knew Duncan Keld better. Not only well enough to write her article but well enough to be sure that he would phone her, keep in touch, stay in her life and want her to stay in his.

He had told her to help herself to the clothes in the chest of drawers in the bedroom, so she went up again and did that. By then the water was warm on the stove. Pattie washed herself and her undies and draped bra, pants and tights over a line she rigged up from a ball of twine she found in a kitchen drawer. There were old black nails in the great beam fronting the fireplace. She twisted the twine around them and hung out her washing.

Then she cleaned her teeth, with toothpaste on her finger. They said it showed a man loved you if he let you use his toothbrush, but maybe she should settle for the comb, and she washed her hair in the melted snow that was soft as silk, and felt silken and sensuous as she knelt in front of the fire on a cushion combing her hair dry.

When Duncan got up she twisted round and looked enquiringly at him. 'Coffee,' he said.

'I'll get it.'

'Thanks.' He saw the washing and his eyebrows shot up, then he eyed her in comic speculation, dressed in his shirt sitting there with her undies all out on the line.

'I'm wearing a string vest and Y-fronts,' she informed him gravely.

'Kinky!'

'Draughty.'

'I'd better boil the kettle,' he said. 'We don't want the wind whistling through your string vest.'

'*Your* string vest.'

He laughed. 'Well, I'm sure it looks better on you.'

He brought two mugs of coffee from the kitchen and Pattie thought he might stay to drink his, but he handed hers over and went back to the table and his work. He was quite unconscious of her scrutiny, she was sure of that, in a world of his own thoughts, but looking at him gave her increasingly pleasurable sensations.

She could feel a rising warmth in her blood that didn't come from the fire, a need stirring in her. She remembered looking across at Michael in the hotel dining room, and feeling nothing at all, but now she had to hold herself back because she wanted to go to Duncan so badly.

She made herself turn away. She pulled on her skirt and jacket over her hotch-potch of clothing. She would go into the kitchen and plan the meal, start cooking, start doing something. My goodness, she thought, I fancy him rotten, and she bit her lip thinking how light and trivial that sounded, and how strong and overwhelming was the hunger inside her, as though she had been starved all her life.

CHAPTER FOUR

THE last dinner party Pattie had prepared for two was for herself and Michael. They had started with avocado pears, then filet au poivre and finally a rather special little lemon mousse, and Michael had complimented her on every dish and held her in his arms afterwards, and said, 'We're two of a pair.'

It was a compliment, he liked her being like him and he would be horrified to see her now. She was a long way from the elegant lady he admired, and he wouldn't go much for the dinner she would be serving tonight either. Which proved they were not two of a pair, because Pattie was going to enjoy it and she had more fun going through Duncan's food cupboard than she had had buying the avocado pears and the steak, although she wouldn't have said no to them if there had been any around.

From the selection there was she decided on spaghetti bolognese, then tinned peaches in a little red wine and the rest of the wine to drink. Her knowledge of wines was limited, so she chose the prettiest label and hoped it wasn't something special that Duncan was keeping by him. She wouldn't ask. She would do nothing to disturb him. She would have to go to the table and touch him before she could get his attention. Or shout. He was immersed in his work again as he was yesterday. Pattie had left the kitchen door open, but glanced through continually and she could sense the intensity of his concentration, but today she didn't feel resentful or shut out, she felt accepted. When he did look up and see her he would probably smile.

Her clothes dried and she changed into them. She would change back into the shirt for dinner by the fire. It was more casual than her jumper and skirt and with a little imagination she could dress it up, give it a bit of flair. Anyhow, it would be good for a laugh. Today she was filled with laughter. She had always had a sense of humour, but she had never been a giggler, but today she was finding things hilariously funny.

Herself stuck up here in the snowdrifts would make a riotous story in the telling. How she had set off to interview Duncan Keld, without checking on the weather forecast, and put her car out of action, and how he spent the first two days glaring at her while she sat by the fire too shaken to eat. But after that they declared a truce and she borrowed his shirt and his string vest and his comb and was given the freedom of the food cupboard.

It was a crazy situation. It made her smile more than once, while she wandered around rediscovering the lodge. She had seen most of it before, but today everything was different. For instance, the big empty room upstairs was no longer just empty, with two trunks, and dust on the floor. It was full of possibilities. It would make a marvellous studio with a portable gas heater or oil lamps. It should be furnished, from auctions maybe. Pattie knew just how she would love to see it, with bright rugs on the floor and comfortable chairs, a studio couch and a big desk.

Duncan wouldn't let it, of course, not even to someone who promised only to use it when he wasn't around, but she would have loved a stake in this house. The newspaper cuttings she had read before she came up here said that he had bought it as a near-ruin and helped to rebuild it himself, putting in the floorboards, mending walls, fixing roofs.

I wish I could have come along then, she thought, and done a little labouring and scratched my name in the plaster in some corner. She had never felt such empathy for a building. It was like coming on her old home again, although there was no similarity at all except that the house where she was born had been old too.

At midday she made more coffee, and cheese sandwiches of wholemeal biscuits, and put them on the table by Duncan's elbow. He looked up with a quick smile and said, 'Thanks, lovey,' and although she knew that meant nothing she would remember the way he said it.

Of course it wasn't just the house, she realised as she ate her own cheese and biscuits in her usual seat by the fire. It was the man. She wouldn't want to be here without Duncan, even if it was the middle of summer or winter, and if they became really good friends he might ask her here again.

She would invite him to her apartment when they were both in London, but suddenly that place, so neat and tidy and lacking any real character, seemed like the home of a stranger. When I get back, she decided, there'll be some changes made. It was a pity her apartment didn't have a fireplace, watching logs burn was wonderfully relaxing.

She relaxed during the afternoon, playing patience with a pack of cards she found in the sideboard drawer, and then prepared the meal and then 'dressed' for dinner. Dressing meant getting out of her sweater and skirt and into the shirt again, with the sleeves rolled up to the elbow and enough buttons left undone to reveal a reasonable cleavage. She felt comfortable and she hoped she looked sexy, and as she hovered over the boiling spaghetti she decided she was getting enough pink in her cheeks to dispense with the beetroot.

It was a lark, cooking like this. She never closed the kitchen door, that way some of the heat from the fire came through and with that and the stove the kitchen was almost cosy. But her real reason was that she could turn from the stove and see straight down the living room to where Duncan was sitting at his work table, and each time she looked it gave her a feeling of security, of everything being all right.

He had lit lamps when the light started to fail, and tonight as well as the one on the table he lit the Davey lamp and she carried that into the kitchen. That was around five o'clock, he was still working at a few minutes to seven, and Pattie was debating with herself how to call him to dinner, without making the break in his concentration too shattering, when the matter was settled for her. She was warming plates on the top of the stove, and she picked up one that had been a little too close to the jet, gave a piercing shriek and dropped it on to the flagstones, where it exploded into smithereens with enough noise for a whole tea-set. 'What the hell are you doing?' Duncan roared.

'What's it sound as though I'm doing?' she yelled back. 'Dropping a red-hot plate. Sorry about all that. I suppose I should have hung on?' She came out of the kitchen, sucking her fingertips and glaring. 'It's five to seven,' she told him. 'Do you want dinner put back?'

'Do we still have a dinner? What was on the plate?'

'Nothing.' If there had been she *would* have been fed up. 'Aren't we lucky?' she said. 'And it's lucky you've got another plate, although I'd better not make a habit of it in case they don't get us out for a day or two.'

Saying that made her feel so much better that she started to smile, and Duncan got up and came towards her, telling her, 'There'll be a snowplough along as soon as it's possible. My neighbours from the farm.' The farm that was a good four miles away. 'You said your family and friends didn't know you were setting off for here, but will they be worried about you?'

'Not for a few days.' Pattie walked back into the kitchen and he followed her and swept up the pieces of plate while she pottered over the stove.

She explained, 'My family's my mother and she lives in California. I'm on holiday from the office and my boy-friend won't panic for about a week.'

'Do you often clear off without leaving him a forwarding address?' He was curious, and it did sound a woolly sort of relationship.

'We don't live in each other's pockets.' She turned off the gas under the spaghetti and added, 'We don't live together.'

'I see.' Do you? she wondered. Well, it's not so clear to me as it used to be. Michael had said he loved her, she had said she loved him, but now she was beginning to doubt if they had ever been together in any way that was deep or meaningful.

She thought of her car as she had last seen it, almost buried in the snow. What with further falls and drifts there wouldn't be much at all to see now, only the very top of the tilted roof perhaps, and she shivered and quipped, 'Somebody's walking over my grave,' and thought that if the car had been her grave in a few months she would have been almost forgotten. Even Michael would soon forget her.

'Let me see your fingers.' Duncan took her hand and her fingers curled instinctively, so did her toes, but he couldn't see them, and she quickly straightened her fingers and he examined the tips and she said, 'It's nothing. Really.'

He agreed, 'You let go in time.'

'A question of timing,' she babbled. 'If you let go in time you're all right.'

But he didn't let go of her at once. He went on holding her hand, looking into her face as though he planned on doing a sketch from memory, and she was staring back at him. He had lines from nose to mouth, two more cutting between his brows. Under the brows his eyes were pitch dark and she could see her tiny reflection in them. She said huskily, 'You've a lot of wrinkles for your age.'

'No, I haven't,' he said cheerfully. 'These are thought lines, a sign of intelligence. How old's your boy-friend?'

'Thirty. You're only twenty-nine, aren't you? Only you look older than Michael.' She was being tactless but while he held her hand she didn't seem able to stop talking, not even long enough to consider what she was saying.

'No wrinkles on Michael?' enquired Duncan.

'Not really, no.'

'A smooth character?'

Smooth, yes, shallow maybe. She said, 'I don't know what you mean by smooth. He's very elegant, very bright too. He's an accountant.'

'A bright accountant should come in handy.' Of course he wasn't impressed, he was smarter than Michael would ever be. He grinned, 'And what would he do if he knew you were stuck out here with me?'

She didn't think Michael would find it funny. When she faced the question, like that, she thought he might be annoyed at her getting herself into this predicament and if he wasn't his mother would have something to say about it. Michael's parents were *very* respectable.

She shrugged, 'It isn't my fault.' She didn't care what anybody thought, she didn't feel the least bit guilty. 'And if he did know what could he do, if even a snowplough can't get through?'

'Mmm.' Duncan seemed to be considering and she said drily, 'What would you do? Drop in by helicopter or swoop down on skis?'

'One or the other.' She believed him, and she felt a stab of jealousy, so she made herself smile and heard herself ask, 'Who is she?'

'Who?'

'The girl you'd pluck out of here?'

'Am I being interviewed?'

'No,' she said, but he probably thought she would use it and he wasn't telling her that kind of thing, because he shook his head at her smiling, and she was glad. She didn't want a name. She didn't want to hear about the girl he would come rushing to rescue. 'It's cooked,' she said, looking at the spaghetti pan.

While Duncan washed his hands she tucked her hair behind her ears, holding the little mirror at arm's length. The soft water wash had left it shiny but floppy. 'You wouldn't have a hairgrip about the place, would you?' she asked plaintively.

'Never use 'em.'

'I thought somebody might have left one.'

'Not with me.'

Pattie sighed at herself in the mirror with her hair falling over her eyes. 'Oh dear! What shall I do with it?'

'What's wrong with it?' It was baby-fine. It needed blow-dry lotions and a mist of lacquer if it was going to hold any style at all.

'Lacks body,' she said, and he burst out laughing.

'I wouldn't say that.' He leered at her appreciatively in her tight-belted shirt, and she laughed, demanding, 'How would you know?' Then she remembered that she had slept beside him last night and blushed while she was laughing, and shook her head to hide it so that her hair covered her face like a veil.

'Let's see,' he said, and Pattie felt his fingers in her

hair with the same shock of sensation as though he had lain them on her breasts. But this was fooling, not a caress. He twisted it gently into some sort of topknot and still holding it, reached to open a drawer and produced a wooden skewer. 'I'm sure I've seen this style somewhere,' he said.

'Portrait of a Victorian skivvy?' she joked, but her mouth was so dry it was a wonder she could speak.

He skewered the bun neatly enough, but the moment he let go the hair slithered down again and the skewer fell out. 'Any more good ideas?' she said.

'We are talking about your hair?'

'What else?' She could laugh at him, flirting and fooling, but inside she melted with longing.

'What we need,' he said, 'is a ribbon.'

What she needed was him and they were here all alone, but nobody was going to come through that door through all that lovely snow, so there was time for everything. 'I'd give a lot for a hair ribbon,' she said. 'Did the girl who didn't leave a hairpin leave a ribbon?'

She was hardly jealous at all now. Whoever the girl was she wasn't here, and from the way Duncan was looking at Pattie he wasn't missing her. 'No,' he said. 'Actually I was thinking of a tie. I do have a tie. I'll get it for you.'

It was grey silk, had a couture label, and looked quite new. 'Did you buy yourself this?' she asked, and he said, surprised, 'No, I didn't, it was a present. Why?'

Because women bought ties for men. Pattie wrinkled her nose at it. 'Oh, it doesn't look what I'd expect you to wear. Too wishy-washy.' In fact it was a beautiful tie, but she had taken a dislike to it.

'Do you want it or don't you?' he asked.

'Yes, please.' Of course she'd have it, she didn't want him wearing it. She asked, 'Do many people buy you ties?'

'No.' He sat on the edge of the kitchen table, legs crossed at the ankles, arms folded, eyeing her.

'Do you wear ties?'

'Funny question,' he said. 'Sure I wear ties, and if this is for that article of yours who the hell cares?'

'It isn't, I'd forgotten I was supposed to be interviewing you, only somehow I can't imagine you sort of spruced up.' The only time she had seen him, before he came here, was when he came looking for her after Willie got his black eye. It had been a wet day, Duncan had been wearing a trenchcoat mac, dark hair blown and unkempt. In the photographs in his file he had looked casually clad, but now he said, 'Don't bother to imagine it. But I do sort of spruce up when the occasion demands. That tie, for instance, I'd wear that on television.'

He did regular programmes that Pattie had always contrived to miss, and she admitted, 'I've never watched you on telly.'

'That's all right, I've never watched you.'

'I've never been on.'

'That accounts for it.' He was laughing at her, but he couldn't know she had resented somebody else buying him a tie and wanted him to say he had no use for it. That really was ridiculous and she smiled. 'But from now on,' she said, 'I promise to watch.'

'And I promise to watch you.'

'Suppose I never get on the box?'

'Who's talking about the box?'

She would like that, if he meant it. She would like

him staying close enough to watch her when they got out of here. She fastened the tie bandeau fashion around her head, knotting it under her hair at the back and not caring how she creased it. If he wanted a grey tie she would buy him one to replace this, then he would remember her when he put it on and not what's-her-name.

'How's that?' She stood still for inspection.

'Very neat,' he said, and stroked her head with both hands, lightly smoothing down the fly-away hairs. It would have been so easy for him to tilt her face and take her lips, and she would have kissed him back with more passion than she had ever shown before. The longing was so fierce in her that her hands seemed to move of their own accord, clasping behind his neck, but still Duncan didn't kiss her, and she couldn't make the next move and kiss him first. Instead her fingers crept up into his hair and she said brightly, 'Yours doesn't slip away. Yours springs back—very strong. I could get a good grip on your hair.'

'One of my best features,' he said. 'Hair to hang on to. You have a beautiful nose.'

'I have?' Her nose was probably one of her best features, straight and nicely chiselled. Michael's was larger but much the same pattern, and he was proud of his profile, she had seen him surreptitiously admiring it in restaurant mirrors.

'Beautiful,' said Duncan. He bent his head and the touch of his lips on hers paralysed her, so that her breath caught and she couldn't move. She would have done. As the kiss became more urgent she would have caught fire, but it didn't. Duncan raised his head again and said, 'Something's burning,' and the sauce was giving out pungent fumes, which made Pattie howl and rush to get the pan off the gas.

'Just spaghetti, is it?' Duncan enquired.

'*No*, oh *no* . . .' She thought it was, though. She could have wept with frustration, because who wanted just spaghetti when she had planned dinner by candlelight? But as the bubbling stopped and she dipped a spoon into the thick meat and tomato there still seemed to be a good layer on top that hadn't caught. 'How do you feel about crispy sauce?' she asked.

'I'll try anything.'

'I'll remember that.' She smiled at him over her shoulder. 'Well, such as it is, it's ready, so please could we lay the table?'

'Which table?'

There was a scrubbed-top table in here, but she wanted the one he was working at. She said, 'I know your papers and things are on it, but I'd put them all back in the same places.'

'I'd rather you kept your hands off,' and she bit her lip at that and said stiffly,

'Sorry about last night, but I'm not going to start flinging typewriters around again.'

'This isn't personal.' He smiled at her. 'I shouldn't think you're a girl who repeats herself, but if we've got to have that table clear I'll clear it.' He collected knives and forks from a cutlery drawer while Pattie drained and dished up the spaghetti and scooped on what was left of the sauce. The table was clear when she carried in the plates, and she said, 'I thought candles would be nice, then we won't see the black bits.'

'Candles?' he said. 'But of course, candles.'

There was a bundle in a kitchen drawer, and two bright red enamel candlesticks on a shelf of the dresser. While he was lighting them she put what was left of the bottle of wine on the table with two glasses, and blew out the lamp. The Davey lamp was still burning in the kitchen and she had kept the fire high enough to illuminate the room, but the flames of the candles danced as Duncan carried them over, throwing shadows on the walls.

'Now that looks interesting,' he said, looking at the plates. 'And what would that be?'

'Oh, just one of my inspirations,' she waved airy hands. 'I get them, you know. Of course an artist is limited by her materials and some people might think this was spaghetti bolognese, but it does have that little extra something. In this case the burned bits.'

He sat down and ate a forkful and announced, 'Which makes all the difference.'

'Oh dear!' Pattie took a hasty taste herself, but even the burned bits were savoury. 'It's not too bad, is it?' she asked, and he reassured her,

'My compliments to the chef.' When he picked up the bottle of wine she said anxiously, 'I'm not an expert, I hope I haven't picked out something that cost a fortune.'

'I haven't got any that cost a fortune, but if I had you'd be welcome, this *is* an occasion.'

She supposed he meant their real first meal together. Breakfast hardly counted and memorable first times were occasions. She hoped this would be memorable for him. It would for her, because of the sheer thrill of eating with a man who made her nerve ends tingle. Maybe it was mainly physical, but it was *good*.

Duncan began to pour the wine, the bottle was about a third empty, and she said, 'The rest's in the pudding. I wouldn't want you to think I've been knocking back the vino. After all, I did help myself to your brandy.'

'So you did.' He raised his glass to her. 'Here's to sobriety,' and the candlelight flickered in his eyes and she thought the devilish touch suited him. It emphasised the Heathcliff look. He said, 'There are candles burning in your eyes.'

'And in yours.'

'We're lit up before the evening's even started.'

Pattie nodded. She must have reflected candlelight over other dinner tables, but she had never before felt this dancing delight deep inside her. Perhaps at parties when she was a child, when she believed in magic. Duncan couldn't be feeling as lit up as she did, but he was certainly in good spirits.

'Where's the vinegar?' he asked. 'Or were you referring to my wine?'

She had been referring to the pickled beetroot she had contemplated using as lipstick. She would tell him about that some time, but now she said, 'I changed my mind. Vinegar wasn't mentioned in your write-ups. Garlic was, that you like garlic, and bangers and mash and seafood.'

'Huh?' He did a double-take and she went on, 'It was in an article about you, in *Metropolitan*. I got your cuttings out of the library when I was told to try for an interview.' She remembered the Jennifer Stanley story and rushed on, 'I know all sorts of odds and ends about you. I know your star sign, for instance—Leo.'

'That's guesswork.' Duncan Keld had been abandoned, aged about twelve months, in the grounds of a Northern orphanage. As soon as his first book made such an impact that became common knowledge, but for a long time now his present life style and character had been colourful enough to fill the columns.

Pattie asked hesitantly, 'Do you ever wonder——? I mean, don't you miss——'

'Parents?' She nodded. 'No,' he said. 'You can't miss what you never had.' He could have been talking about something too trivial to matter, and that seemed sad to her. 'You didn't find your charm?'

If she had found it she would have been wearing it, even if the chain had broken and she had had to thread it on a piece of string. She said, 'It must be outside,' and wondered if he was reminding her that losing her father after fifteen years had been more traumatic than if she had never known him.

'No,' she wanted to say. 'We had wonderful times and he loved me very much, I always knew that.' Maybe somebody's heart broke when they left their baby son and ran away, but the rejected child would never know for sure that he had ever been wanted.

Still it didn't seem to have hurt him. Not one man in a million had as much going for him now as Duncan. She drank a little wine and said, 'I read about here, this place. Did you really rebuild it?'

He looked around with pride of ownership. 'I restored it. You should have seen it. Another year or two would have been too late, any building here would have been a new building, but I got in just in time. When that first book took off I ploughed in all the royalties and put everything back.'

'I wish I'd been here,' she said. 'Oh, I *wish* I had!'

'I wish you had,' and he looked at her almost as though she had been around, helping to mix the mortar, handing up the bricks. A sharing look. He'll let me come again, she thought, and was enclosed in a glow of contentment that contained herself and Duncan and the whole room.

She said, 'This is your second home?' Perhaps she could pretend it was her second home too.

'My first. I spend more time in the flat, but this is my bolt-hole.'

'Where you can be alone.' Only she had gate-crashed, and it was wonderful that he no longer minded. They were like old and loving friends. She felt she could ask anything, tell him anything. She could even reach across the table and touch his hand or run her fingertip over the small crescent-shaped scar on his cheekbone. She didn't touch, but she felt it would be all right if she did. They ate and talked, and Duncan told her, 'It probably dates from early days when I slept in a dormitory and ate at a long table and always seemed to be in a crowd.'

'You're not happy in crowds?'

He shrugged. 'Oh, I don't mind getting jostled, most of the time.' Nobody would push him far, that was for sure. 'I travel around, getting material, meeting people.' Pattie knew all about that, but when he smiled and said, 'Then I come here,' she felt that she knew him better than any of the other journalists who had written those articles.

'Do your friends come?' she asked.

'In the summertime.' Probably he only came alone when he had work to do. When the lodge had been pointed out to her last summer there had been cars around it.

'Do you bring girls?' she asked, and wished she hadn't. 'Well, of course you do.'

'In the summer,' he said. 'There aren't many women who'd go for this in wintertime.'

Rubbish, she thought. They'd go for it fast enough if you were here, and she drawled meaningly with glinting eyes, 'Oh, I'm sure there are compensations for the isolation.'

'But of course.' His grin made her giggle, hinting at all sorts of lascivious goings-on. 'There's me.'

'You take their minds off it, do you?'

'Try me!' But while she laughed, over the sound of her laughter she heard the wind rising. She had heard it before in the big chimney and rattling the windows, but suddenly it seemed to have a voice like a lost soul, sighing and sobbing and indescribably lonely.

She listened, head on one side, and Duncan watched her, listening too. She could imagine the white wastes out there, and at last she said, 'It sounds as if it's coming from a long way away.'

It died down on a sigh, but a few seconds later rose again and went on and on, and he asked suddenly, 'What's your mother doing in California?'

Now that was a long way away. That was as far as another world. 'Living there,' she said, 'with her husband. He's a doctor, he's very nice.'

'A doctor and an accountant?' He was probably laughing at her.

'Oh, I'm like you,' she said, 'I'm never ill.' In the last ten years she had never gone down with anything more serious than 'flu, but she wasn't like him physically, she was nowhere near as strong. Nor mentally, come to that.

'Do you see them?' he asked.

She said eagerly, 'Yes, of course. Last year we met in the south of France for a couple of weeks. They got married two years after my father died.' She didn't suppose Duncan was interested in dates and details, but while he listened, dark eyes fixed on her, she felt compelled to go on talking. 'She loved my father very much, but she needs a man around. She needs looking after. She's one of those fragile blondes with big blue eyes who look as though a breath of wind would blow them away. And she never looks a day older. On holiday last year everyone took us for sisters. Next year somebody is going to ask if I'm big sister, and by the time I'm thirty I'll be Mum.'

She was smiling, because it was a smiling matter and she was proud of her pretty mother, who loved her and kept in touch, and often said their home was Pattie's. After her father died things would have been easier for Pattie if her mother had shown more strength of character and less selfishness, but nobody had expected that. Barbara Ross's helplessness was part of her charm, and it seemed natural to her friends that fifteen-year-old Pattie should be the supportive one. Some of them remarked that Pattie was showing less emotion than they would have expected at losing her father, none of them had seen her shed a tear, but Barbara wept. Barbara had the nervous breakdown and everybody's sympathy.

Pattie smiled now and said, 'She's quite exquisite, you have no idea,' and Duncan said wryly, 'I think I probably have,' and she wondered what he meant by that. Was he so constantly on the look-out for characters for his books that you only had to describe somebody and he could visualise them?

The wine and peaches went down well, and they carried the dishes into the kitchen and dumped them in the sink. 'They'll be there tomorrow,' said Duncan.

Pattie didn't want to wash up now, heating water and hanging around. She wanted to sit down and talk some more and then she wanted Duncan to kiss her and shut out the wind's lonely song.

The wine bottle was empty, and he opened another, but she demurrred, 'I think I've had enough.'

'You not driving, are you?' he said.

'Nope.' It didn't really matter whether she kept a clear head or not. If she was at risk she didn't care.

'Right, then.' He took the bottle and their glasses to the fireplace, set them on the floor and sat down on the goatskin rug, leaning back against the old armchair.

'Comfy?' she asked.

'Come on down.' He reached a hand up for her. 'You get the best view of the fire from here.'

'The flagstones are hard,' she said, although she had sat on the rug herself and it was a good thick shaggy one. It must have belonged to a mountain goat from some place where there was a nip in the air.

'You can lie on me,' he offered.

'Wait till I go numb.' She sank down beside him and he put an arm around her and she relaxed with a little sigh. Staring into the fire might not be good for your eyes, but it was very pleasant. Beneath the outer shell of the logs was a glowing labyrinth. When you squinted you could imagine it was tiny rooms, and she asked, 'Do you see pictures in the fire? Places?'

'What do you see?' Duncan turned the question on her.

'A tiny shiny shell-pink palace.' She drank some of her wine and started to describe it, the rooms, the corridors, pointing as she talked and leaning forward. The warmth of the wine and the fire were making her dreamy so that she could almost imagine herself in there, walking through a fairyland, and when Duncan asked, 'What's your home like?' for a moment she couldn't think of a single attractive feature to brag about.

Then she said with a little laugh, 'Tidy. I'm a tidy girl.'

'Is that a fact?'

She might not look very well groomed now, but it was a long time since she had lived in any kind of disorder. She explained, 'There wasn't much money after my father died. We couldn't afford domestic help and my mother was ill. She really couldn't do anything, so I did the cleaning and tidying after school. I suppose it became almost an obsession with me.'

She had never realised that before. She had just gone on in the same way when she moved into her own flatlet, after her mother remarried and flew off to America and then into the bigger apartment she rented now. By then it was a way of life, but it had started as a desperate attempt to preserve her home so that if her father should return everything could go on again as it used to be.

She said shakily, 'I've got a phobia about cleanliness. That's why I hated not being able to have a good wash. It made me feel ill. I can't stand grime.'

'In that case,' said Duncan, 'come here.'

He wiped her cheek, very gently, with a white handkerchief, and she saw a smear of soot. 'That's what I get for sticking my head up the chimney,' she said. 'Are there any more?'

He smiled. 'Call them beauty spots.'

'All right.' She snuggled up against him. 'Oh, it's nice here. I never knew anywhere that was so comfortable.' The comfort was in him, in the support of his arm around her and the dizzying awareness of his warm body so close. She wanted to stay here with him for ever because outside there was so much loneliness. The wind sobbed in the chimney and she raised her head and looked into the dark questioning eyes that held hers.

For a moment neither spoke, then Duncan must have read the inner loneliness in her, because he said gently, 'Shall we go up?' and she whispered,

'Yes. Please.'

CHAPTER FIVE

THE cold was waiting at the top of the stairs. Heat was supposed to rise, but Pattie started shivering when she walked into Duncan's room. He was carrying a candle. Downstairs he had blown out the second candle and set up a spark guard in front of the fire, while Pattie sat on the goatskin rug, hugging her knees.

She wasn't thinking clearly, she wasn't thinking at all. She was letting herself drift on a wave of pure sensation where there was no tension and no stress.

When he held out a hand to her she scrambled to her feet, so euphoric that if he had led her into the snow she would probably have gone with him.

But she shivered now, getting out of her boots and feeling the chill creeping over her. In the lamplight the windows were shimmering white, you could see neither sky nor stars. She looked away from Duncan, but she had no urge to get away, and she undressed quickly and slipped into bed, pulling sheets and coverlet up to her chin.

The bed was ice-cold, making her gasp, starting her teeth chattering. 'This is like falling into a snow-drift. I could freeze to death in here!'

He laughed, 'Not with me around,' and the lamp went out and he was beside her, pulling her close, and the length of his hard lean body against the yielding softness of her own stirred her so that she could no longer hear the wind for the singing in her blood. Masculine, and strong, and infinitely tender, his lips and hands wooed her and warmed her on a rising surge of passion, until she was on fire for the touch and the taste of him, with a wildness she had never even suspected. The whole world seemed shut out. She was coming to life, gloriously and raptur-ously in the soft silent night, blossoming like a passion flower under the mind-blowing expertise of his love-making . . .

It was morning when she woke and the first thing she saw was Duncan, sitting up, propped on one elbow, looking down at her. Joy filled her. She could never remember waking up feeling this happy. It was like the scene in the *Wizard of Oz* film where the black and white world blazes into colour. Just looking at his face, and liking it so much, was wonderful.

The right face, the right time, everything right.

They both smiled, slow smiles as though they were savouring each other's nearness, and then Duncan bent to kiss her bare shoulder and run a stroking hand down her arm, and her senses shivered and thrilled. She would have been willing to stay where they were all day, but his hand strayed no further, and she wriggled a little higher, getting head and shoulders above the bedclothes, wondering what time it was.

The windows were still frozen. She squinted across at them and said, 'We could be sealed in here for ever.'

'What a way to go!' He needed a shave and she didn't mind. A man's rough cheek could be very sexy. She had never kissed a rough cheek before, but she tried it now, and it was arousing—it nearly drove her wild—and she thought, my goodness, I mustn't carry on like this, I must show a bit of self-control. So when Duncan started to kiss her back she shifted slightly and joked, 'Maybe the Ice Age has come and they'll find us in a hundred years, lying here, smiling.'

He grinned at her, 'How about that for a head-line?' Their breath frosted over them, and she hoped the fire was still burning downstairs, although she was sure Duncan could get it going again in no time.

'How about a cup of coffee?' she suggested.

'I do like a practical girl!' He gave her another kiss, very chaste this time, on the forehead, and she wondered if that was true, about the girls he liked. He must have liked Jennifer Stanley for a while, but apart from being ravishingly pretty Pattie couldn't recall that she had had any special talents.

She was much prettier than Pattie, but her affair with Duncan was a long time ago. He probably hadn't seen her for years and now she was getting married, so it wouldn't matter to Pattie how pretty she was. There would be other girls, out there, who had claims on Duncan, but today nobody could bother Pattie. He was dressing fast because of the cold, and she thought inconsequentially, he isn't all that hairy. He had said he was a hairy feller, but his back and shoulders were tanned and smooth as bronze. She could see the ripple of moving muscles, and imagined him asking her to sun-oil his back on some palm-fringed beach. Even when he had pulled a vest over his head and knotted a sweater round his neck she knew exactly what he looked like under the clothing, and she smiled as she began to wriggle into her own clothing under the sheets.

He grinned across at her, 'Aren't you scared you'll get something on upside down?'

'It'll be a novelty,' she said.

'Do you usually dress under the bedclothes?'

'I don't usually get dressed in sub-zero temperatures.' But she would have dressed herself this way in a heatwave. She was still very slightly, and ridiculously, shy, and as soon as Duncan went downstairs she threw back the sheets and put on the rest of her clothes at speed.

Duncan had put several small logs on the embers and they were crackling and flaring within minutes. In front of the fire Pattie changed shirt for sweater and skirt, warmed her hands and face, and then followed him into the kitchen where he had a kettle almost boiling on the gas jet.

It was coffee from a coffee bag, but it had never

tasted better, rich with flavour so that she smacked her lips over it like a child with a lollipop. She was hungry too, cooking bacon, and breathing in the aroma.

'I'm not a breakfast eater,' she told Duncan who was shaving at the sink. 'Except on holidays I'm a cup of coffee and a half of grapefruit.'

He reached one hand around her waist, running fingers over her ribcage and making her squeal—she had forgotten she was ticklish—telling her, 'That's why you're so thin, you need feeding up.'

She wondered if he liked plumper girls. 'It could be because you starved me for the first two days,' she said. She was joking, of course, she hadn't eaten because she wasn't hungry, but now her appetite was sharp. She was cooking eggs too.

'Your fault.' Duncan had the little mirror propped up on the window ledge ledge above the sink and Pattie wondered if she could say, 'I don't mind if you don't bother shaving.' But he was doing this because she was here and it was a compliment. 'What did you think I'd do if I caught you in the cupboard?' he asked.

She had been stubborn and angry. And she had been afraid. 'Well,' she said, 'you were angry with me for coming here, and for that gossip item.'

She saw him frown in the mirror, although he went on with his shaving, and she bit her lip and asked, 'Did he really jilt her because of that?'

'Yes.' Everyone in Fleet Street knew that was the reason, but Pattie had hoped he might say, 'I don't really know why.' But he was definite. 'It started the quarrel that split everything wide. His family were a lot of stuffed shirts. They put pressure on him and the story lost nothing in the telling.'

She bit back the questions she wanted to ask about Jennifer Stanley, how long and how strong had the affair been between them? Had he seen her since? Had he ever loved her? But she knew she could never pry into that area of his life and that she would be taking a chance if she asked him any deeply personal questions. He could close up, the barriers could come down again, and all their lovely intimacy could end.

She said instead, 'She was well rid, don't you think? A man who lets his family decide against the girl he wants to marry—she could well have regretted marrying him.'

'Maybe,' said Duncan, tight-lipped, and that was the subject closed, and it wouldn't be Pattie's fault if it ever came up again. She was anxious to forget it. She finished cooking the breakfast and Duncan finished shaving, then they took the food into the big room and ate in front of the fire.

He produced a small transistor radio, at which she shrieked, 'I didn't know you'd got that!'

'There's a lot you don't know about me, lovey.' He was joking, but it was true, and she would have thought he'd have brought the radio out before, if it was only to play some music. But when he came here to be alone, perhaps he wanted quietness too. They were getting the nine o'clock news now and she grimaced, 'Doesn't get any better, does it?'

'Not much does,' he agreed, and she thought, except me. I think I've improved in the last two days. She needed her hair styling, and her make-up and some decent clothes, but all that was surface stuff. Inside was what counted, and inside she had never felt happier or stronger, and never so alive.

The weather report was snow. Countrywide falls, with the usual resulting chaos on rail and road. Villages cut off and farmers striving desperately to save their livestock. But a thaw was forecast and Duncan said, 'Thank God for that,' and Pattie's heart sank.

Duncan's neighbours on the moor were farmers and she could understand him putting himself in their position. But while she was saying how terrible it was, what a loss, what a worry, she knew that she would be happy if the snow stayed for a few more days. He was here to work, he didn't mind being snowed in, but as soon as a way opened he would expect her to leave. At least she supposed he would, although she could stay a little longer if he asked her.

They finished breakfast, listening to the radio, and then she asked, 'Would music bother you? May I leave it on? Please say if it would disturb you.'

'If it would disturb me I shouldn't have brought it down,' he said. 'You're not one of these who have to have it blaring full blast, are you?' As she shook her head he said, 'Of course you're not.'

'Quiet, you mean? A bit dim?' She had never been dim, she had always been intelligent. But she had been one of the quiet ones, reserved and retiring, and now although she laughed she was wondering how she seemed to him.

He smiled at her, 'I mean there's nothing impaired about your hearing, nor your mind, nor your eyes, nor any sense or part of you.'

'Thank you,' she said demurely. 'You seem in pretty good working order yourself.'

'Yes, ma'am.' He gathered the plates to take into the kitchen, leaned across and kissed the tip of her nose, 'And you haven't seen anything yet!'

'I can hardly wait!' She put on a look of wide-eyed innocence and he chuckled,

'It's a temptation, I can tell you, but talking of work——'

'Oh yes,' she said, 'so I'll take the plates. Perhaps you'd let me have some of your paper and lend me a pen, and later on I can do some writing too. But you carry on now and pretend I'm not here, and then I shan't feel I wrecked your schedule by barging in on you.'

She would have loved it if he had said, 'I don't want to work. I'd rather sit here and talk to you.' Better still if he had taken her in his arms and kissed her properly, because a thaw was on the way and their time together like this had to be limited. But he did say, 'You're no wrecker,' and looked at her with an expression she couldn't quite fathom before he went across the room to his working table.

She thought about that look while she was in the kitchen, washing up after breakfast and then washing herself and combing her hair. Duncan didn't have a particularly expressive face, but she was almost sure the look was half way between tenderness and amusement.

There were no immediate signs of a thaw. When Pattie put on the sheepskin jacket and went outside the snow still seemed hard, although her footsteps crunched a trail around the yard and the wind was still bitterly cold. Somewhere out here she had lost her pendant, and she looked on the ground and peered into the woodpile as she pulled out a few more logs. No luck, but it would turn up eventually and in the meantime the snow wouldn't hurt it. Gold

didn't rust, old gold coins and jewellery came up
from the sea-bed as shining as the day they went
spiralling down and down through the water.

She *wished* that Duncan had taken a break. This
morning everything seemed sharper and brighter and
more exciting. She would have liked him out here
with her. She would have liked to build a snowman
or throw snowballs. She cut a pattern of two huge
interlocked hearts in the snow with the shovel, then
wrote her initials in one and D.K. in the other with
her finger. Then she decided it looked a bit too
soppily sentimental and scuffed it all out again. But
it made her smile, and she thought, I don't just fancy
him, I'm falling in love with him, so what shall I
cook us for supper tonight?

She was beginning to feel quite proprietorial about
the kitchen. She had the radio playing quietly, and
she sang along, very softly, with some of the tunes, as
she sorted through the cupboards again and set out
the ingredients for tuna fishcakes on the table. She
scrubbed two large potatoes from a bag of potatoes
under the sink, and whipped up a mousse with a tin
of evaporated milk and a tin of strawberries. That
took a long time, with only a fork for a whisk, but
today she had time. Then she put it outside in the
snow to set. She was a good cook, when she was
entertaining she used exotic ingredients and tried out
adventurous recipes, but here it was all convenience
food. When they were back in London she would ask
Duncan round for a meal and set something really
mouthwatering before him. And she would make
herself so beautiful. She would buy a new dress. That
would really knock him back, because he had never
seen her glamorised.

She did a lot of daydreaming that day. Nothing seemed impossible, and all her dreams included Duncan. He had put a pad of lined foolscap writing paper and a fibre-tipped pen on the armchair, and Pattie sat in front of the fire and tried to do some work. Usually she used a typewriter, a pen slowed her down, and she had no clear idea what she intended writing. Her assignment up here was to interview Duncan, but she couldn't start on that. He'd know what she was doing somehow even if she didn't show it to him, and it would put him on the defensive. She couldn't even make notes about him, and she didn't want to. This was personal, sweet and secret. All she had learned about Duncan she would never tell a living soul.

So she wrote letters instead to friends with whom she kept in touch by mail, cheerful and chatty, not even mentioning where she was, because if she did she would have to say who she was with, and she would like it best of all if that never came out. She wasn't thinking very logically today or she would have known that there wasn't a hope of getting herself, let alone her car, back to civilisation without questions being asked. But today she wrote letters as if she was still in her apartment, or snatching a spare half hour at work.

Even to her mother she wrote as though the clock had stopped some time last week. She had always censored her letters to California, never dwelling on anything remotely distressing. 'Your mother has a very sensitive nature,' they had told her when her mother broke down after her father's death, and Pattie had never sent a letter that could disturb her.

Not that there was anything to worry about in this

situation, but she had long ago got out of the habit of confiding in her mother. She didn't want anyone to know. Not yet. She looked across at Duncan and remembered what a critic had said about his last book—'a writer of powerful passion'—and that applied to him as a man too.

'Dear Duncan,' she wrote, 'Thank you for your hospitality. It's been a pleasure knowing you. Such a fantastic, unbelievable pleasure. If I was told I had to stay here with you for ever I wouldn't mind, because I can't think of anything outside this house that could make me as happy as you can make me. And that's why I love you, I think . . .'

She looked across again and met his eyes and smiled and looked away, and turned over the page on the writing pad. 'Dear Joan,' she wrote, 'Lor', what weather we're having!' and a few minutes later surreptitiously tore out her letter to Duncan, rolled it into a tight ball and tossed it to the back of the fire.

She brought in the same lunch as yesterday, cheese between wholemeal biscuits and a fresh mug of coffee. He thanked her, as yesterday, with the same quick smile, and she almost pleaded, 'Can't you take the afternoon off? We could go for a walk if we were careful where we put our feet and you know where the drifts are. Or we could stay in. I'm sure we could think of something interesting to do if we stayed in.'

But he had turned back at once to his papers, and Pattie chewed on her knuckle and went back to the fire, building it high until fountains of sparks went soaring up the chimney. No, she decided, I'm not in love. That would be stupid when you're obviously not crazy for me, but I do like you more than any other man I ever met, and some time in the future I

could be in love with you and you with me. And
right now is pretty good, so I mustn't be greedy.

There was an old pack of cards in one of the
drawers in the kitchen and she played Patience
during the afternoon, with the cards spread out on
the flagstones, herself sitting cross-legged on the
goatskin rug. Michael's mother played Patience. She
had taught Pattie during a rainy Sunday afternoon
when Michael took Pattie home for the day. Pattie
had said she couldn't play Patience, but she could
read the cards, having written an article on fortune-
telling the week before, but Michael's mother was
having none of that. She had called it tampering
with the forces of nature, and Pattie smiled now,
remembering.

Probably Michael and his parents would call
Duncan Keld a force of nature. Too much strength
and raw talent for their tastes. Anyhow, knowing
how to play Patience was coming in useful, although
Michael probably wouldn't have recognised Pattie,
and suddenly she realised that she could hardly remember his face.

Her hand stilled, in the action of laying one card
on another, and she frowned. Of course she would
remember him, he looked like she used to look, and
she willed him back into her mind in all his immaculate elegance. But for a moment he had been as
shadowy as though it was ten years instead of a few
days since she had last seen him . . .

She played around with the food, preparing
dinner. She couldn't wait for Duncan's watch, on
the kitchen table, to come round to seven o'clock
when he would be finished with work for the
day, and she spun out the preparations for the

meal to pass the time.

There was a selection of tinned and packed soups. Somebody had once told her that tinned lentil soup improved out of all recognition if you added a little curry powder, and she was surprised to find that it did. She baked potatoes, cut in half lengthways, scored criss-cross and spread with butter and a little salt and dried mustard, and carefully fried the fish-cakes heart-shaped. It should have been an ingenious meal, but when she went out to collect the mousse she had a nasty shock.

Something had got in ahead of her. The bowl had been tipped up, some of the contents lapped out, and all around, and heading back into the hills, were paw prints. Pattie had no tracking craft. A wildcat? A fox? What did they have out here? Whatever there was must be hungry. 'I wish I'd left you something else and kept this in the kitchen,' she muttered at the retreating tracks, and went back indoors to open a tin of rice pudding.

She had lit the lamps when the light began to fade. Once you had seen it done it was easy. And she had changed back into Duncan's shirt, which meant keeping the fire high but did make her feel more glamorous than her sweater and skirt.

At ten to seven she went across and put a hand on his shoulder and said, 'Hi.' A current of warmth seemed to flow into her from the contact with him and she let her hand fall reluctantly. 'It's ready,' she said, 'but a fox ate the mousse.'

'What ate what?'

She grinned, realising how odd that had sounded. 'Strawberry mousse. It should have been the pud-ding, but I put it outside to set, and I think it was a fox. You don't have yetis round here, do you, with very little feet?'

He chuckled. 'If we do this is the weather to bring them down from the hills.' He began to put his papers into a drawer and Pattie asked, 'What's the book about?'

'I'll send you a copy.'

She would have liked him to tell her about it now. The tape-recordings had all been factual notes and dull listening, but Duncan's books were never dull. The only one she had read was the paperback in her case in the car, but she knew that from review head-lines and hearing other people's opinions. When she got back home she would read them all, and perhaps he was remembering that she was supposed to be interviewing him and didn't want his current work discussed in her magazine. She might have told him that she wasn't thinking of herself as a journalist these days, but she had hoped that he knew that.

He shut the wide drawer under the table into which he had put papers, tape-recorder, half a dozen fibre-tipped pens, clicked the top on the typewriter, set it down on the floor against the wall, and asked, 'What have you been writing?'

'Letters,' she said.

Now that the wind had dropped perhaps it meant that the thaw had started, and soon she would have to leave. She asked, 'Would you like the news on the radio?'

'Not particularly.'

She had turned off the radio about an hour ago, but now she wanted to fill the silence that might mean that the snow was melting. She switched on to music and let it play softly in the background, and while Duncan washed she set the table, lighting the candles.

They had burned down about half way last night. They looked bright and colourful in their scarlet candlesticks and she wondered, will they gutter out tonight or be blown out? She brought in the bowls of soup and as Duncan sat down opposite her he said, 'This could become a habit that's hard to kick.'

Oh, I *hope* so, she thought fervently. He filled the wine glasses from the second bottle they had hardly touched last night and smiled at her, and she picked up her spoon and started drinking her soup, feeling more at home than she did in her own apartment. Secure and content, and at the same time filled with a passionate longing for the man who was facing her.

He wanted her too. She knew from the way he looked at her. Their smiles, their talk, all seemed to Pattie to carry a deeper meaning, although it was a hilarious meal. Duncan told her about some of the catastrophes that had cropped up during the restoration of the lodge. He described the men who had helped him so that she could see the whole gang. Joe with the red hair, sharp as a ferret; Bert the brickie, built like a tank, whose wife had left him to join the army, and Tom and Dick and Jerry. That was when he first made friends with the family at the nearest farmhouse who had lent him a tractor and learning to drive it he had knocked down a wall five minutes after the last brick had been laid.

Pattie talked about her early attempts at interior decorating. The Christmas after her father died she had thought it might cheer her mother if she colour-washed the lounge. So she roped in a couple of school friends and the three teenagers managed to cover themselves as well as the walls. She went into giggles, recounting it. 'I got the drip sort of paint, of course, and we did the ceiling and the paint kept dropping on our heads. So then we put on headscarves and Sarah—she was a lovely big bouncing girl and a bit of a disaster area, she was always knocking things over, barging into things—was up the ladder, and her headscarf fell down over her eyes and she fell off the ladder clutching the paint pot. It took hours to wash Sarah and the carpet, but we had it all finished by night.'

'Did your mother like it?'

She laughed again. 'That's the funniest part of all—she never noticed! I'd even changed the colour, from white to pale coral. She'd been taken out by friends, she went straight to bed when she got back. Next day was Sunday and by teatime I had to tell her, and then she said it was nice.' She went on smiling. 'Mind you, I told the girls she was thrilled to bits.'

She had been gesturing as she was talking, and Duncan caught her hand, fingers locked, holding palm against palm, and again she felt warmth and energy like a life force flowing into her. We fit each other like trees whose roots are entwined, she thought. I could grow with him.

She said, 'It was funny.'

'Of course it was,' he said, but it was as though he knew why she had chosen Christmas to try to make the house special. Because—except for the year before—her father had never missed coming home for Christmas. She had known he was dead, but she couldn't accept it. She and her school friends had joked together while they were doing the painting, but that Christmas Day had been bitter for Pattie.

She asked, 'Do you ever come here for Christmas?'

'No,' he said.

She had always spent Christmas with friends, last Christmas with Michael and his family. She could see this place with logs burning and a tree sparkling, and a good old traditional dinner which could be prepared in the stove quite easily with a little planning. She murmured, 'It would be super.'

'With the right company,' he said, and Pattie almost knew that she would be here next Christmas. He got up. 'Let's have coffee by the fire.'

'I'll make it.'

'You cooked the meal, I'll boil the kettle. Fair division of labour.'

She pulled a face at him. 'I bet that's what you said when you hit the wall with the tractor!'

After they'd carried out the dishes she left him in the kitchen, came back and pulled off her boots. They were soft leather, but they were beginning to rub, and she couldn't borrow Duncan's shoes like his shirts and pull them in till they fitted. The flagstones struck chilly to her stockinged feet until she reached the rug in front of the fire, and then she selected another big log and heaved it on and sat watching it burn.

It was almost like a Yule log. She would love to spend Christmas here. Since she was fourteen she had never enjoyed Christmas much, but a Christmas with Duncan would be something to look forward to, something to remember. With Michael's family it had been organised from morning till night—presents, parties, everything in good taste because his mother had done the organising. Pattie had been grateful, and bought extravagant gifts, and been glad when it was over.

That was only last month, although it was last year, and there was nearly another year to run till Christmas. She wondered what this year would bring her, and she knew what she wanted. She picked up the pack of playing cards as Duncan came back with two mugs of coffee and asked him, 'Shall I read the cards for you?'

'If you insist.'

'You're not superstitious?'

'No.' Of course not. She couldn't imagine him touching wood or avoiding ladders, or relying on anything but his own skill and strength to make his luck. Nor was she superstitious really, although her pendant had been something else, because that had been her father's goodbye gift.

'Fair enough,' she said, 'I'll read my own.' Duncan sat in the armchair, Pattie sat on the rug dealing herself five cards, face down, with theatrical flourish. Then she put fingertips to temples, closed her eyes and breathed deeply. 'Calling up the powers,' she explained.

'You want to watch it,' he advised her. 'A yeti might answer.'

A faint moaning came from the chimney, the wind seemed to be rising again, and she intoned, 'I hear you. What do the cards foretell?' She turned up a three of hearts and said, 'That's a friendly little card. Threes are letters, you know.'

'I didn't know.'

'Stick around me,' She fluttered her eyelashes. 'You'll learn things.'

'Boasting again,' he said.

There's not much I could teach you, she thought,

but it's lovely to laugh with you, and I would rather be here tonight than be crowned Queen of England.

The next card was the Jack of Clubs and she held it at arm's length. 'Well?' asked Duncan.

'Man,' which was obvious. 'Medium, sort of.'

'Michael?' he suggested.

'Could be.' Three of hearts would do nicely for Michael, a low-powered card but amiable. 'Looks like Michael,' she agreed.

Duncan peered at the one-eyed Jack, 'Strewth!' and she grinned.

'Figuratively speaking, you idiot. Actually Michael looks a bit like me.' Duncan's eyebrows rose. 'I mean he's got the same shaped features, the same sort of hair. And in a lot of ways he has the same tastes.'

When he asked, 'Isn't that boring?' she hesitated. A few days ago she would have said, 'Not at all,' but she thought now that it was. Never to argue, never to spark anything from each other. She shrugged. 'It seems to suit Michael, he's always saying we're two of a pair.'

'It sounds more like bookends than a flesh and blood couple,' said Duncan, and that made her smile wryly, while she protested, 'It's been a steady relationship.' But a little short on magic. Michael was no spellbinder the way Duncan was, there was no black sorcery around him.

She sat hugging her knees, chin resting on them, looking into the fire, remembering the last time she had seen Michael. 'I didn't mean to come up here when I set off from home,' she said. 'Michael had gone down to the Cotswolds for a few days, on business, and I was going to arrive at the hotel and surprise him. I booked myself in and went to the dining room.'

She turned another card and grimaced at the six of spades, and Duncan asked quietly, 'Wasn't he alone?'

She shook her head. 'No, it was nothing as dramatic as that. He was having dinner with these other men, talking business, and he didn't see me, so I watched him and I just didn't want to go over. So I went up to my room and I left in the morning and I didn't bump into him again.' She bit reflectively on her thumbnail. 'And I honestly don't know why it suddenly seemed a good idea to go on driving and come here and try to interview you. I'd phoned your number in London earlier and a man said you were up here.'

'That would be Harry, he and his wife are the caretakers.'

'Well, he said you were in Yorkshire and not on the telephone, so I thought it had to be here.'

The wind *was* rising again. It sounded as though it was trapped in the chimney. 'How did you find it?' Duncan was asking her. 'It isn't that easy,' and she explained,

'I passed here last summer, on holiday.'

'With Michael?' He wasn't smiling, but he seemed amused and she supposed she had made her relationship with Michael sound a bit of a joke. It hadn't been. There hadn't been many laughs in it at all. She said, 'With some girls from the office. One of them pointed the lodge out and I've got a good sense of direction. If I've been anywhere once I can always find my way again.'

'You always know where you're going?'

She looked up at him, her eyes bright and enquiring. 'In life, you mean? Ah, that's different. Do you?'

'I think so.' He paused for a moment. 'Barring the unforeseen.'

The unforeseen for her had happened after she lost her pendant, and found herself weeping in Duncan Keld's arms. There had been a changing of direction for her from then on, because now she felt she could only be happy if he was travelling the same road. She fluttered her hands over the cards and chanted, 'Consult the oracle and the way ahead will be made clear,' fooling because she was shaken to realise how much he could influence her future plans.

She turned up a ten of spades and shivered, 'Nasty!'

'Reshuffle them,' Duncan suggested, and she acted horrified.

'You can't do that. That's cheating!' But it was as well she wasn't a believer because she was holding a card of ill omen, and she looked at it with distaste until he twitched it out of her fingers, said, 'Don't let a piece of cardboard hex you,' and spun it into the fire.

'Now you've spoiled the set!' She watched it catch alight, then her head jerked up and she turned to Duncan, gasping, 'What's that? Not the wind,' because the noise in the chimney was rising to a roaring, crackling crescendo.

'The chimney's on fire!' He was on his feet as the first lump of blazing soot fell, followed by half a dozen others, bouncing over the piled up logs in the fireplace like fireballs. The goatskin rug began to smoulder and he rolled it fast and pushed it away, then

started dragging everything combustible back, armchair, cushions, while Pattie threw the logs she had
brought in, and dried, and stacked neatly beside the
fireplace, out into the room.

Puffs of acrid smoke were belching out, and when
she touched the stone of the chimney breast it seemed
red-hot. That last big log she had put on was leaning
against the side of the fireplace with soot glowing all
around. She held her breath and peered up into the
swirling smoke and Duncan roared, 'Get out of there,
you silly cow!' and pushed her aside, dumping a
bucket of snow on to the fire that hissed and steamed
and then went on burning merrily.

'But I did it, I did it!' she wailed, and he snarled,
'What do you want, a citation?' and dashed outside
again. Soot was still falling and the only water available was snow. Patti grabbed the washing up bowl
and ran into the yard with it. Out here was like a
fireworks display – flames and sparks shooting out of
the chimney, blazing stars drifting down into the
snow. Sparks landed on Pattie as she scooped, and
she rushed back to empty her bowl, then out again
and back again, passing Duncan and screeching,
'What else can we do?'

'Nothing, except put the soot out as it falls and let
it burn itself out up there.'

'We couldn't get up to the chimney?' He didn't
bother to answer that, just gave a snort of exasperation, and it was a daft suggestion. Of course they
couldn't. There probably wasn't a ladder, the roof
would be a skidpad and what could anyone do up
there without water and hose?

Finally they damped down the logs in the grate
and then put up the spark guard to hold back some

of the soot falls, and stood guard with snow. Pattie said miserably, 'It's all those logs I've burned, I'm so sorry.'

Duncan grinned, 'You don't do things by halves, do you? They'll probably see this in town and think we're sending up distress rockets.'

'Will they?'

'I doubt it.'

The flagstoned floor was running with melted snow. Nothing was likely to set on fire down here, but now she ventured to ask, 'Do you think the timbers will catch?'

'I think we should thank our stars we're not thatched,' he said. 'The cards didn't give much warning, did they?'

'I *was* running into a bad luck patch.' She chewed her lip, looking at the scattered, sodden pack. 'And now I'll never know what the last card was.'

The fire in the grate was a black streaming mass. Everything seemed to be smoking or steaming, but the bright burning soot had stopped falling, and Duncan stepped forward to peer up the wide chimney.

'You told me to keep my head out of there,' Pattie muttered. 'I suppose it's all right to be bullish but not cowlike about these things.'

'It's nearly over.' He smiled at her. 'You should see yourself!' and she was as relieved that he could joke about it as she was that the danger was passing. She ran into the kitchen and came back with the little mirror and held it in front of his face. He was sooty black so that his teeth flashed startlingly white, hair on end as though he had been up the chimney, acting as a flue-brush. He dropped on one knee, arms outflung, and burst into song, a passable imitation of Al Jolson: 'I'd walk a million miles for one of your smiles.'

'Don't Mammy me!' Pattie gurgled, and he got up again.

'No, you're right, it would never work.' But the giggles died in her at once because the place was a shambles, and even now there could be sparks smouldering among the old beams. The stones of the chimney breast were cooling, but she was still fearful. She said huskily, 'I could have burned the place down.'

'The chimney should have been swept before. It wasn't all your soot, you know.' He wasn't letting her take all the blame, but she was anxious for more reassurance, pleading, 'It is going to be all right? Nothing's going to crack or burst into flames?'

'I shouldn't think so for a minute, but we daren't re-light the fire for an hour or two, so it's going to get pretty chilly in here.'

Pattie had already started shivering. Some of it was reaction, and she had been running in and out of the snow in her stocking feet—how was that for panic? She hadn't even stopped to put her boots on. She'd have to get out of her tights and into her boots, but now she crawled towards the old armchair and almost collapsed into it, holding her head in her hands, whispering, 'I couldn't have borne it if anything had happened to this place. That would have been too dreadful.'

'Drink this,' he said.

'Not this much.' She looked at the measure and shook her head, but he went on holding out the glass to her. He had another in his hand and she was too shaken to argue, so she took it and took great scalding gulps getting it down. She certainly needed something to steady her.

Duncan sat beside her in the big chair and she huddled against him. Not just for warmth but because it was good that he was still holding her when this could have thrust them apart. Of course it wasn't all her soot, but she had kept up a fire like a furnace ever since she came. Of course if the lodge had burned down it might have been different. He might have called her more than a silly cow then, and she had a picture of scorched and blackened ruins against the white hills, and turned her face into his shoulder and tasted soot and singed wool.

But the brandy was making her sleepy, and when he said, 'We'd be warmer upstairs,' she said, 'I could sleep for a month.' Waves of exhaustion were sweeping over her, so that she swayed as she stood up, and kept her eyes closed, climbing the stairs.

Duncan probably carried her, because she seemed to get up there with hardly any effort, and the pillow smelt clean under her cheek. And her last conscious thought was, All this soot, all over us. How am I going to wash the sheets?

CHAPTER SIX

PATTIE's head was throbbing when she opened her eyes. It was all that brandy, and probably the smoke too. She opened her eyes the merest slit, and closed them wincing. Then she took another peek and saw

Duncan standing at the bottom of the bed, fully dressed and clean-shaven, his hair looking damp as though he had just washed it.

He was smiling broadly, and that seemed rather unfair when she felt so rotten. But she smiled back, weakly, and he asked, 'What would you like best in the world?'

Her voice wobbled like her smile. 'Surprise me.'

'A hot bath.'

'Second best.' Her voice was getting stronger and he said,

'Ah, you're lovely,' and came over and kissed her, and that made her feel better and she mumbled against his mouth,

'What I'd like first best is two aspirins. I've got a hangover, my head is killing me!'

He burst out laughing. 'And I thought you were putting me top of the list!'

'Not at the moment.' Pattie touched her temples gingerly. 'It's all that brandy you gave me on top of the wine.'

'Treatment for shock. You need it.' Duncan was still laughing, and she lay back on the pillow her head thumping.

'It wasn't a nightmare, was it?' she asked. 'We did have a fire?'

'The chimney. Yes.'

'What's it like down there?' She could imagine it. The floor would still be wet, everything would be all over the place and smelling of smoke.

'All right,' said Duncan.

'How long have you been up?'

'An hour or two.' He brought her a couple of paracetamols and half a glass of water, and she gulped and swallowed. 'Go to sleep again,' he said, and although she felt she ought to be up and doing she wouldn't be much use in this state. So she murmured apologetically and then drifted back to sleep.

Next time she woke the headache had receded. The pain was no longer agony. She sat up groggily and saw the soot stains on the pillow and remembered how filthy she was. There were tiny burn marks on the shirt she was wearing, that had been from the sparks outside, and when she ran her fingers through her hair little frizzy scorched ends came away. She threw back the sheets and grimaced.

She was still in the tights in which she had run into the snow, her feet were still damp, and she got out of them and put on a pair of thick socks she had found in the chest of drawers, then she went downstairs. She didn't expect it to be as bad as she'd left it last night, but she wasn't prepared to find everything back to normal. The fire was burning brightly and nobody would have known anything unusual had happened, there wasn't a sign or a smell of soot.

Duncan called from the kitchen, 'Coffee?'

'Oh, please, and you did mention a hot bath.'

He chuckled, 'Up to it, are you?'

'I'd better be.' She went into the kitchen. 'Look at me, and your bed is revolting!'

'Now that's not a nice thing to say. A man could get a complex being told things like that.' Pattie grinned.

'Well, I tell you most of the soot's rubbed off on the sheets. You do have a change of bedding?'

'Several.'

'Thank goodness!'

Besides the kettle there was a big two-handled container boiling on the stove, and the tin bath was out of its cupboard. Pattie hadn't seen the pan before, but there was enough hot water in there for a shallow bath. 'You can have it in front of the fire,' said Duncan, and she went on grinning,

'Oh, you are so good to me!'

'Oh, aren't I just?' He patted her cheek and she went weak at his touch so that she had to lean against the kitchen table. Because he was making coffee, he wouldn't want her hanging on to him. And he had bathed and she was still sooty; and it was too early in the day to expect him to take her into his arms and make love to her.

She drank her coffee while he carried the tin bath to the front of the fire and poured in the hot water. There was a large white towel and soap on the arm-chair, and he brought in a bucket of snow and said, 'Get it down to the right temperature and you wouldn't get better treatment in a five-star hotel.'

'Certainly not better room service,' she joked. She took off the socks she had borrowed, and began to cool down the near-boiling water with handfuls of snow. She was shy about stripping, although Duncan wasn't watching her. All his attention was centred on his papers. It didn't seem to bother him having a girl taking a bath in the same room. If the circumstances had been reversed she would have found it confusing but perhaps he was used to it. After all, that was how these old tin baths were used, for ablutions in front of the fire. Perhaps that was how everybody bathed in this house, including visitors.

Once in the water she concentrated on soaping herself liberally, including her hair. It was the first time she had examined herself for bruises from the car crash and there were less than she had expected.

Her tan was fading, and turning a dingy yellow, she would need some extra solarium sessions to restore that. She wondered if Duncan's tan came from spending time under hot suns or because he was naturally dark. A touch of the gipsy perhaps, or Spanish blood. She was sure it didn't come from a bottle or a sunlamp, as hers did.

Soon the water began to cool. If she had been offered another kettle to warm it up she would have lain here soaking a little longer. But she didn't fancy disturbing Duncan, and what with the bruises and the fading tan she decided she looked a bit like a plucked chicken, so she hopped out and swathed herself in the enveloping towel.

As soon as she was dressed she would heat a kettle to rinse the soap out of her hair, and she began to towel herself dry, and then Duncan looked across and asked, 'Finished?'

'Yes, thank you.'

He dragged the bath out through the kitchen and the back door, and Pattie shivered as cold air blew in, and hastily donned bra and pants. As he came back, towards the fire, towards her, she pulled the towel round her once more, and asked, 'Any sign of the thaw out there?'

'I wouldn't have said so.'

Good, she thought. She said, 'It's lovely in here, and we must have the cleanest chimney for miles.'

'We've got the only chimney for miles.'

'Then there's no contest.' Then she shivered again as his hands cupped her shoulders under the towel, and his fingers ran down her spine, but this time with pleasurable anticipation. As he drew her closer she lifted her face for his kiss, the hunger in her rising sweet and sharp, and when she heard the shouting she almost screamed '*No . . .!*'

She would have given almost all her worldly goods to have been mistaken, but Duncan had heard it. He stood, still holding her, listening, and in the silence it came again, his name, men calling, 'Duncan, hey, Duncan!'

Pattie ran the tip of her tongue between her dry lips. Her throat felt dry too, and so tight that it was aching. 'Your friends have come for you,' she said.

'It sounds like it.'

He went towards the front door. It seemed to her he went in slow motion, that everything was happening slowly, caught in a time lag; that even the flames in the fireplace had ceased to flicker. Then as he touched the door she jumped into action, dragging on the tights that she had brought downstairs to wash, grabbing her skirt and sweater.

'It's John and Barty Brunton,' said Duncan from the front door. 'You'll like them.' He waved and called, 'Hey!' back and went to meet them, closing the door behind him, and Pattie, dressing frantically, thought, I don't like them very much right now. Right now I'm pretty sure they're no friends of mine.

She struggled into her boots and jacket and then ran into the kitchen and began to tug the comb through her dripping hair. It would have been more sensible to have stayed where she was, by the fire, and gone on rubbing her hair with the towel, but she was suddenly anxious to look tidy.

She had sleeked down her hair and buttoned her jacket when the front door opened again and Duncan came in with two other men. They were muffled up in identical anoraks and gumboots, short and stockily built, with blunt-featured ruddy faces.

They had both been talking at once as they came through the door but when they saw Pattie they stopped dead, rooted to the spot and silent. A strange woman was obviously the last thing they had expected to find here.

'Pattie,' said Duncan, 'this is John and Barty. They followed the snow plough.' She smiled and wondered if her smile looked as false as it felt and said, 'Hello.'

'Pattie Ross,' said Duncan.

'Pleased to meet you, Miss—er——' the older man took a quick look at her left hand, 'Miss Ross. I was just saying to Duncan here that we saw the chimney last night, only we weren't sure it was just a chimney then, and when the snowplough started getting through first light on the top road we followed in the car because we didn't know what was going on up here.' He cleared his throat, looking embarrassed, and rushed on, 'This young dog never mentioned having company. Why didn't you bring the young lady to supper with us the other night?'

The son was looking even more puzzled. Obviously Duncan had been at the Bruntons' farm the afternoon that Pattie arrived. One of these men must have driven him back to the darkened lodge that night, while Pattie was sleeping before the fire in the old armchair, and by next morning the lodge was well and truly cut off from the outside world. Yet here she was. So how had she managed it? Unless Duncan had brought her here earlier.

She said hesitantly, 'It is a little complicated.'

'Not at all,' said Duncan briskly. 'Miss Ross is a journalist. She came to interview me while I was at your place. Her car went off the road just round the bend of the track and is still down there, and she got in here through the kitchen window.'

'And she's been here ever since?' said the younger man.

'That's right,' said Duncan.

'Car out there?'

'Yes,' said Pattie.

'Surprised there hasn't been a hue and cry,' said the younger man. 'Well, you don't look much the worse for it.'

It was like a dig in the ribs. He didn't believe that Duncan had no idea Pattie was waiting for him that night. He thought they had planned to stay up here together, that he and his father had blundered on a secret rendezvous.

The expression on the faces of both men was amused and apologetic. 'Mum's the word,' they were saying without speaking, and Pattie thought, now they've got over the first shock they're not all that surprised. I'm not the first girl who's stayed here. And she heard herself ask, 'Do you think you could get me back to Grimslake?'

There was a moment before they answered, long enough for Duncan to have protested, 'What's the rush, you're still on holiday, aren't you?' But he didn't, and the older man said, 'Yes,' and the younger said, 'Sure we can, if that's what you want.'

What she wanted was Duncan to put an arm around her and say, 'Thanks for checking, but we're fine. Now the snowplough's through we'll be seeing you before long, but not for another day or two.'

But he didn't. What he did do was bring the sheepskin coat and put it on her, and ask about the livestock situation and agree with both farmers that the snow storms had been a wicked business. Pattie had the feeling that he couldn't get her going fast enough. It was as though the rescuers had arrived that first morning when the prospect of having her underfoot was infuriating him. Perhaps not quite like that. He wasn't angry with her now. He was friendly, cheerful, but in no way was he loving.

'We'd better see if we can get some of the stuff out of your car,' he said.

'Are you coming too?' That hope was immediately dashed by his emphatic,

'Where would I be going? I'm home.'

She wondered if he meant to be cruel, although he smiled as he said it. But of course he had never told her to think of the lodge as her home, that had been one of her crazy dreams. She said, 'Well, I certainly would appreciate getting my hands on a few of my belongings,' and told the Bruntons, 'I left my case in the boot, and my coat and handbag are in the car, and my wallet and keys and everything are in my handbag.'

Trudging along the track wasn't easy. The snow didn't seem to be melting very fast, it was still firm underfoot. 'Where's the thaw, then?' asked Pattie as she stepped outside, and the men all smiled at her and she blinked because the cold made her eyes smart. 'Doesn't it make your eyes smart?' she said when she sniffed, and she could feel Duncan looking at her. She would have hated him to think she was crying because her eyes were moist.

Inside she was crying. Outside she kept walking and smiling. Even when they were walking heads down into the cold wind her set expression was cheerful. She might look like an idiot, but nobody would suspect how miserable she felt.

'There's my car,' she said, pointing down, 'sticking out of that drift.'

The Bruntons whistled 'Phew!' together. The older said, 'We can get it out for you when the snow's gone, but I don't see how anybody could haul her up yet awhile. You must have had a bumpy ride lass.'

'I did wonder how far down I was going,' she admitted. She could have still been lying there, and she should feel grateful for being alive, and she would later. But Duncan was half way down the bank now and all she could think was how anxious he was to get rid of her.

She stayed where she was. The younger man slithered after Duncan and they were both wading through waist-high snow. She watched them burrowing around the car with their hands, struggling with the frozen door and dragging it open. They brought out her handbag and camel coat, shaking the snow from both, and she cupped her mouth with her hands and shouted, 'My gloves are on the back seat!' She might as well have the lot while they were down there. The car could be stripped before it was hauled back on to the road. It could be a wreck. She remembered the splintering, crashing sounds of that nightmare fall, how the car had finally ended up on its side, and resigned herself to its loss.

It didn't seem to matter much. She had lost more than that. The dark man down there, although he had never been hers, had left a void that ached like a wound.

It took a long time to prise open the boot. The older Brunton stamped his feet for warmth, standing by Pattie, and looking around, fretting at the time being wasted, and she said, 'I'm sorry about this.' Then he grinned and told her,

'That's all right, lass. Can't leave your baggage down there, can we? By gum, though, you were lucky.'

'Yes, I was,' she said, and wished she had gone down with the men because during all the activity of digging into her car she and Duncan would have been talking, helping each other. When they got out her case, she might have managed to laugh and say, 'Well, I'm set up for a few more days now, and I don't exactly have my interview. Could you put up with me just a little longer?'

But when they brought her belongings to her there was no chance. Duncan said, 'Here we are, then, they'll dry these for you at the farm.'

'Of course,' said the younger Brunton. 'Stay as long as you like.' So Duncan had been fixing her up with shelter. He wasn't risking her suggesting she went back to the lodge. She said brightly, 'How kind of you, but I think my best plan is to catch the first London train back home. Your Yorkshire moors are magnificent, but I've had enough of them to be going on with.'

'The train would be from Darlington,' said the older man. 'But no rush, surely. You'll need a good meal and a night's rest after this.' And they set off again, the two younger men carrying Pattie's luggage, except for her handbag which she clutched to herself.

The Range Rover stood on the swathe of the road that the snowplough had cleared. The plough had gone. It was out of sight now, somewhere over the hills. There was no sign of traffic or life. They had walked almost silently from where Pattie's car had crashed, and now the younger Brunton opened the Range Rover door and her case was put on the back seat and she got in beside it. 'Right, then,' said Brunton senior, getting into the front passenger seat while his son settled himself behind the wheel.

'Goodbye, Pattie,' said Duncan. 'See you some time.'

'I expect so.' She managed a wide smile. He didn't touch her, much less kiss her. He waved goodbye as though he was seeing off a guest who had almost overstayed her welcome.

All the same, when the car drew away and she looked back at him, still standing there, she very nearly cried, 'Please stop!' and jumped out of the car to run and fling her arms around him. But it was as though he read her thoughts, because suddenly he went striding fast over the hard-packed snow without turning round again, although she watched through the back window of the car until he was out of sight.

The Bruntons' farm was the one she had passed on her way to the lodge, looking different under its blanket of snow although the yard around was churned up and blackened. There was another car parked by the back door.

Pattie noted the sticker 'Press' on the windscreen and began to ask if they could possibly take her on to Grimslake, where she might get a taxi to Darlington, when the back door opened and two women came hurrying out.

After that she was overwhelmed. The women were 'Mother and my wife Janet,' and when they heard where Pattie had come from they were fascinated.

They took her inside to the fire and put a cup of tea in her hand, their eyes shining and curious. Duncan was all right, the older Brunton explained, it had only been his chimney on fire. And Miss Ross was a lady journalist who had got herself snowed in at the lodge. 'A friend of Duncan's?' asked Janet, a pretty girl with brown curly hair and big brown eyes. Her eyes looked huge at the moment, they were so wide, and Pattie's own lids felt as heavy as lead. She would have liked to close her eyes and shut them all out.

'I went up there to interview him,' she said. 'And the snow came.'

A balding man who had a glass of what looked like whisky in his hand and who was staring hard at her had to be Press. 'Jack Robson, *Broad Ridings Mercury*,' he said, when his eyes met Pattie's. 'You're a journalist?'

She told him her magazine and he grinned. 'And you've been snowed in with Duncan Keld. Just the two of you?'

'Yes.'

'I'd like to read your article.'

'Buy the paper,' she said.

'Better be getting on.' He grinned again and drained his glass. 'Any sign of any cars or anything up there?'

'Only mine that we saw,' said Pattie.

He went out of the room with the men. She supposed he was getting his story from them. Duncan was well known. There would be a mention in most nationals about his home being cut off in the snow, and she knew there was no way of keeping her own name out of it.

'But I thought Duncan's young lady was that nice

little fair-haired girl,' said an old lady, sitting in a rocker, whom Pattie hadn't noticed till then, and Janet sounded flustered, 'Oh, *Gran*, that was last summer—you know Duncan.'

'I'm not his young lady,' said Pattie. She wondered about the blonde who must have come up here and been introduced as his girl, and she asked, 'Please could I use your bathroom?'

'Of course my dear,' said Mrs Brunton. 'Do you want your case?'

Somebody had brought Pattie's luggage in from the car. The case was damp. When she opened it everything felt clammy, and she took out her make-up bag, then snapped the lid shut. She would wait until she got back to her apartment before dealing with that. Her hair was still almost as wet as when she left the lodge, and as Janet led the way to the bathroom she explained, 'I was just washing my hair when your husband and your father-in-law arrived.'

'They might have given you time to dry it,' said Janet. 'A thing like that could give you a shocking cold. By the way, how well do you know Duncan?' She was obviously madly curious. 'I mean, he was here the night before the snow started and he said he was going to be working. Barney takes him up, you see, then goes back after a week or so and sees if he wants anything or if he wants to come down. He said he reckoned on staying about a month this time.' They had reached the bathroom door. 'But he never said a word about you being up there,' Janet continued.

'He didn't know I was,' said Pattie.

'Oooh!' Janet pulled a gleeful face. 'If I wasn't a happily married woman I'd wish I'd thought of that myself.' She gave a hoot of laughter, and Pattie knew it was useless insisting that she had only been pursuing Duncan for an interview.

She would have stayed on at the lodge if he had given her the chance, but he hadn't. She wasn't even sure if she was going to see him again, so there was really nothing at all between them, and she couldn't stay in this house where people were going to talk about him, and ask questions about him. She said, 'I have to get to London. Have you any idea when I could catch a train?'

'You don't want to wait a bit?' Janet sounded disappointed. 'You're more than welcome to a bed.'

'That's very kind of you, but I must go.' There was nothing to wait for. Duncan wouldn't be coming. Pattie would be asking to be hurt if she ever started waiting for Duncan. She said, 'I must look terrible, I'll just put on some make-up,' waved her make-up bag and went into the bathrom.

When she saw her bedraggled reflection she could understand why Janet hadn't contradicted her about looking terrible. I'll bet the nice little fair-haired girl was a knock-out, she thought; and she washed her face and began to smooth on moisturiser. She was fairly satisfied with her appearance when she had finished. There was colour in her cheeks and lips, and her eyes looked brighter with dark sweeping lashes and highlight on the browbone. She would fasten her hair back with a scarf, there were a couple in her case, and altogether she was almost the old Pattie.

But not entirely. Getting snowed in at the lodge with Duncan had made changes in her, altered her attitude to a number of things. She hated leaving him because it had been good between them. It couldn't have meant so much to him or he wouldn't have been so willing to say goodbye, but it was a new experience for Pattie. She had never, as a woman, been so relaxed or uninhibited, and she was grateful for that. Even if they didn't meet again for years she would always think of him with affection.

They told her she was lucky the trains were running once more, and she was certainly lucky that Janet was willing to drive her to Darlington, although all the way Janet would keep chattering about Duncan. He had been a good friend of Barney's ever since he first came looking at the lodge and decided to rebuild it. 'Of course nobody had heard of him much then,' Janet declared, driving carefully over the still treacherous roads. But now he was famous and his neighbours were proud of him.

She talked about how he and Barney were mates, about visitors to the lodge, and Pattie longed to ask more about the girls who came. Like who were the special ones? But it was none of her business. It was Duncan's life. She was on her way to pick up the threads of her own life and her involvement with Duncan Keld was probably at an end.

When her train arrived in London it was dark. The heating in the carriages had been erratic and she had regretted leaving Duncan's coat behind at the farm and wearing her own, because her own had been damp. It was still damp. When she stepped out on to the platform everything seemed damp and cold and miserable.

She stood, with her case at her feet, looking up and down as though somebody might be there to meet her, which was stupid when nobody was expecting her.

She took a taxi and climbed the stairs to her flat, passing shut doors. Her phone was ringing and she fumbled with the key, hurrying, and ran in leaving her case in the passage outside. Then she stopped and turned and came back for her case and let the phone ring itself out. She wasn't up to talking and explaining yet. She needed a cup of tea, she wanted to get the heating going. She didn't admit, even to herself, that because it wouldn't be Duncan on the phone she didn't want to answer it.

It rang again in about ten minutes. By then she had her tea, and she had turned the electric fire on high so the room was warming. She was sitting by the fire and she got up reluctantly and went to the phone.

'Pattie?' said a woman's voice. 'This is Clare René.'

Clare had taken Pattie's job on the gossip column. Pattie hardly knew her, and it was surely no coincidence that she was ringing now. 'We've just had a call from our man in Yorkshire,' Clare explained. The reporter Pattie had met at the Bruntons' farm had been making a little lineage money. 'He said you've been holed up in Duncan Keld's hunting lodge for the last five nights.'

'Four days,' said Pattie, and Clare laughed, 'It's always more fun to count the nights. When are you seeing him again?'

'I wouldn't know,' said Pattie wearily. 'And don't turn this into a big production, because it isn't.'

'You honestly did go up there just to interview him and you both got snowed in?'

'Yes.'

She could imagine Clare's incredulous expression when she said, 'Really? Well, I know there was a time he was threatening to black your eye like poor old Willie's, but I thought things must have changed for the better between you since then.' She meant she'd presumed that Pattie Ross and Duncan Keld were having a discreet affair, and Pattie said slowly and clearly,

'I never saw him again after that barney in the pub until the other day at the lodge.'

'So there's no romance at all?'

Pattie wanted to put the phone down, but if she did that would be interpreted as no comment because there was something to hide, so she said crisply, 'Never set eyes on the man in the last twelve months, I told you.'

'So you did,' said Clare. 'All right, I believe it. You didn't go up there together. But you were together, and there was nobody else, and he's a virile sort of chap and you're a good-looking girl, so what did you do to pass the time?'

'He'd gone there to write,' said Pattie, 'and he did. I cooked a few meals and did some writing myself. We weren't up there for a month, you know. Oh, and the chimney caught fire.'

She heard Clare laugh. 'Only the chimney?'

' 'Fraid so,' said Pattie.

'Sounds as though you missed your chance, sweetie,' said Clare. 'I wish I'd been in your shoes. And,' she added pointedly, 'your bed.'

'You'd have been welcome,' said Pattie lightly. 'I was glad to see the snowplough.' In fact she hadn't seen the snowplough, and when she'd heard the voices of her rescuers her heart had sunk like a stone.

'Know what I think?' said Clare. 'I think you're a very dark horse.'

But Pattie wasn't being drawn. 'I can't imagine what gives you that idea,' she said, and this time she did say goodbye and put down the phone.

She knew that call had set the pattern of other calls, so she took the phone off the hook and began to unpack her case, draping clothes around to air. Duncan's two paperbacks were in the case, but she didn't think she would read them just yet, although her holiday wasn't over. She had more than a week left before she was due back at the office and she remembered her plan to redecorate. It would take more than a roll of wallpaper to turn this place into a home, she thought, and was astonished at herself because it *was* her home and she had always liked it well enough.

But tonight she was lonely in it. She was starting a streaming head cold to add to her miseries. There was a harshness at the back of her throat and her eyes, and she took aspirins and hot milk and went to bed, and she was lonely there too. She lay huddled in the darkness, wrapping her arms around herself, racked by a terrible feeling of loss.

She had a crush on Duncan Keld. This raw, aching yearning had never happened to her before, and it would pass because it would have to. But there were times when she thought the night itself would never pass, the luminous fingers of the clock were hovering around four before she finally fell asleep.

She woke to the ringing of her doorbell and sat up sneezing, in two minds whether to answer. The ringing stopped while she was groping for a dressing gown, but started again almost at once, and she went slowly to the door.

Michael looked as dapper as ever, carrying brief-case and umbrella and with a pained expression. He said testily, 'Your phone's been engaged a hell of a time.'

'I took it off the hook last night,' she explained, and stepped aside to let him in. As he passed her he asked, 'Have you seen the morning paper?'

'No.'

He opened his briefcase and took out a newspaper, turned it to Willie's gossip page and spread it flat on the table. There was a photograph of Duncan and a smaller rather smudged one of her that Pattie remembered from a snapshot. She read, 'Marooned by snowdrifts in a hunting lodge on the Yorkshire moors for the last five days, Duncan Keld, TV personality and best-seller writer, and glamorous reporter Pattie Ross. Pattie it seems went along to interview Duncan for her monthly column and had to stay until the snowploughs got through. Asked how they passed the time all on their own she said, "Writing, and the chimney caught fire." Pattie is now back in town, but Duncan remains in the hunting lodge. Can't wait to hear his version of the fire.'

'What on earth is that all about?' asked Michael, not unreasonably.

Pattie sneezed again. 'I did go up there to get an interview.'

'To the middle of the Yorkshire moors? In *this* weather? What made it so urgent?'

She saw through the window that it was trying to snow again. So much for the thaw. Duncan should be safe from interruptions this time, and she must stop remembering what it was like inside the lodge and feeling homesick for it. She said, 'It wasn't snowing when I went.'

'You never mentioned it to me. I was hoping you'd join me.' Michael's eyes were narrowed. 'Mother,' he said, 'thinks you were very indiscreet. She doesn't like Duncan Keld's books.'

Pattie felt her lips twitching. 'If she'd mentioned that sooner I'd have told Roz I couldn't possibly consider interviewing him.'

'I think you were indiscreet,' said Michael, as though that clinched it. 'What did happen up there? That's what folk are going to ask. These days they'll all take the worst for granted and it's going to make me a laughing-stock.'

Michael would hate anyone sniggering around him. He was very sensitive to ridicule, and she said cynically, 'Then you'd better keep away from me until the fuss dies down. Give it about a month. Nobody's going to remember it much longer than a month.'

'That's nonsense,' he snapped. 'Of course they will.' He seemed more concerned about what people were going to think than with what actually happened and she almost told him, 'There was one bed up there, and on three nights we shared it,' but that would be as bad as slapping him across the face. She couldn't hurt his pride like that, and she said, 'I didn't plan to stay. I was going to book myself in at the Plough in Grimslake.'

'I know that.' But he still sounded aggrieved. 'And I know that nothing happened between you and Keld.'

'You do?'

'Of course I do. No man would get far with you in

just a few days. You've got too much self-respect. You're not one of the wild ones, you're more on the frigid side.'

'Thanks a lot,' she said, and he hastened to explain, 'It's a compliment. My folks have always said you're a lady.'

'Even this morning?'

'They thought you were indiscreet, that it was an odd thing to do, but they know there's no question——' Michael left it at that, frowning and shaking his head, then checking his watch, 'I'm due in the office, I'll see you later.'

As he went to kiss Pattie goodbye she sneezed and he backed away. 'Sevenish?' he asked. 'I'll call for you.'

It was the kind of day she had expected. Everybody who knew her seemed to have read the paragraph. As soon as she replaced the phone it started ringing, and although she explained that she had intended her visit to the lodge to be fleeting she doubted if any of them believed her. They were surprised all right, but most of them took Clare René's attitude that Pattie Ross had been a very dark horse, managing to keep her affair with Duncan Keld such a secret.

Even at the office, where they knew she had been told to interview him, they couldn't understand why she had taken off for the Yorkshire moors in such terrible weather, and without telling a soul. And what had gone on while she and Duncan were snowed in alone? Roz chuckled, 'It ought to be a smashing article, although I don't know how much of it we can print,' and Pattie wondered how she could write it.

She was as sure as she could be that she had seen the last of Duncan for a long time, and she was pretty sure that before their paths crossed again she would be over the worst of her infatuation. The depression of her first night had lifted by next morning, so that when Michael left her she grimaced and shrugged and answered the continually ringing phone without getting too niggled by it.

She didn't care much what the callers thought. She stuck to her story, that there had never been an affair and there wasn't now, and that was true enough and she had no regrets.

She was still on holiday, and she got out and about. Usually with Michael in the evenings, although she knew that that relationship was near its end.

Even before she had gone up to the lodge it had been dawning on her that nothing in Michael reached down to the depths in her, and now she was grateful for the cold that had developed into sniffs and sneezes keeping him literally at arm's length. He was something of a hypochondriac and these days the most he attempted was a peck on the cheek.

She woke each day with a feeling of anticipation, and wherever she went around London, eating out, wandering through shops, parks, city streets, she kept scanning faces. Not searching for anybody in particular of course, just looking.

A week after she returned from Yorkshire Willie phoned to tell her that Duncan was back in his London apartment. Willie had rung him, and been told that he had no plans for meeting Pattie, and Pattie confirmed that, 'We've no plans—no, why should we have?'

But she had four days left of her holiday and she

suddenly decided she would redecorate after all, and bought some Laura Ashley wallpaper and set about prettying up the living room in a Victorian pattern of small rosebuds. She ate at home too. She hardly went out at all, and the phone rang several times and every time her heart missed a beat, but it was never Duncan.

Not that she was waiting for him to ring, that wasn't why she was staying close to the phone. When she got back to work and got down to the article then she would have to contact him, and by then she would have recovered from the schoolgirl crush that was still filling her nights with fevered dreams.

But she met him again on the last weekend of her holiday, at the press showing of an exhibition of sculpture. The artist was beginning to make his name in rugged rock carvings, and Pattie remembered reading that Duncan had bought some of Jack Saker's early work. She had wondered if Duncan might be at the exhibition, but she had gone along because she was interested in the sculptures herself.

As she walked into the gallery she looked for Duncan, and in that moment all her self-deception vanished. She had come hoping to meet him, for no other reason, and when she saw him in the middle of a group at the far end of the room, she knew that she had been searching for him ever since they parted.

The room was fairly crowded, but when he turned and looked at her nothing in the world could have kept her from him. She almost started running. She could feel herself drawn like steel to a magnet. He never moved, he didn't even smile, but his power over her was frightening.

I love him, she thought, and the realisation filled

her with dismay. I really love him, but what he feels for me isn't strong enough to make him walk across this room.

CHAPTER SEVEN

Duncan didn't come to meet Pattie. Instead he turned away for a moment almost as though he would rather not have seen her, and that stabbed her to the heart, but she couldn't hold back, and by the time she reached him he was smiling.

They were being watched, but she didn't care, although she still had enough wit left not to make a spectacle of herself and keep her greeting light. 'Hello there,' she said, with a big bright smile. 'I didn't expect you back in town just yet. I thought you'd be at the lodge for weeks yet.'

She thought he was glad she hadn't thrown her arms around him, because he relaxed and grinned at her, his voice as cheerful as her own. 'Oh, I made very good time with the work, got on very well.'

'With no distractions?'

He laughed. 'No more chimneys setting on fire, you mean?'

'What else?' Pattie ached to get really close to him. She wanted to touch him so badly, but a number of the folk here knew him and some knew her, and this meeting was going to be talked about, so she stood with folded arms, head back, trying to look nonchalant.

'I didn't know you were interested in Saker's work,' he said.

'I'm a journalist, I go where I'm sent.' She hadn't been sent to cover this exhibition. She had flashed her press card at the door, but she had come for her own reasons.

'So you do,' he said. 'You were sent to interview me and look where that landed you!' They shared the joke, smiling into each other's eyes, then Duncan said, 'Come and meet Saker,' and put her hand through his arm.

Pattie gripped a little, to reassure herself that there was muscle and bone beneath the sleeve and this wasn't just another dream. She pretended she had moved awkwardly and needed to steady herself, but holding on to Duncan was making her weak at the knees. If he kissed her now she would have clung to him in a passionate embrace for as long as the kiss lasted, and she wouldn't have given a damn about the staring faces. Nor for the cameras.

'There he is,' said Duncan. A man with a bushy beard was waving his arms at the biggest piece of rock in the gallery. He had quite an audience already, and Pattie said, 'How about you telling me about them? You must know what they're about. You've bought some, haven't you?'

'A couple of small ones,' he said. 'I like rocks. They're attractive creatures.' He stroked the nearest piece and when Pattie looked closer she could see the skill of the carver, because it was still a rock and yet it had an animal quality, as if the spirit of the rock peered out. Once she started discovering the hidden figures and faces it became like a game. They went from one exhibit to another and it was fun. Being with Duncan anything would have been fun. She was very talkative, very at ease.

'What happened about my car?' she asked.

'It's still where you left it. It's still snowy up there, don't you ever listen to the weather reports?'

'No too often. What about my letters? I left them behind: Did they get posted?'

'They did. Did your article get written?'

'Not yet. I'm back at work on Monday, then I shall start on it.' He gave her an old-fashioned look and she grinned. 'Would you care to censor?'

'Too right I would,' he said.

So she would have a perfect excuse for seeing him again, and she had to turn her head to hide the elation that must be shining in her eyes. 'This is my favourite,' she said. 'The cat rock.' It was apricot-coloured—Cotswold stone, hunched, with the suspicion of a feline smile and slanting eyes. She couldn't make up her mind whether it was malignant or friendly, but it was one hundred per cent watchful. Once you had stared straight at it its gaze seemed to follow you.

'You know,' she said, 'I could live with that.' She put her hand on the head, and he covered her fingers with his own and her heart swelled with delight.

'Ah,' he said, 'but could it live with you?'

'Are you suggesting I'd be hard to live with?' She had been so happy that she was babbling anything that came into her head, but after she heard herself say that she flushed scarlet, especially when Duncan said, 'I wonder.'

He was joking, of course, he hadn't wondered anything of the sort, but he looked down at her and asked quietly as though it was a serious question, 'Everything all right?'

'With me? Sure, I'm fine. Except for this snuffly cold you might have noticed.'

'That's what you get for running around barefoot putting out chimney fires!'

She said breathlessly, 'I loved every minute of it,' and he asked,

'What are you doing this evening?'

She started to say, 'Not a thing,' then clapped a hand to her mouth and mumbled, 'Damn, damn, damn, I've got Michael and his mother coming.'

'That sounds cosy.'

She had been avoiding Michael's family ever since her return from Yorkshire. But today his mother was in town, doing some shopping, and she had invited herself round to Pattie's for the evening. Pattie wasn't looking forward to it. She knew there would be a heart-to-heart, even with Michael hovering around, because in Mrs Ames' book nice girls never got themselves into gossip columns.

'Can't you put them off?' Duncan suggested.

'Oh, I wish I could,' she said fervently. 'But I don't think she'd enjoy being paged through Harrods and told to go home for her tea. I could see you tomorrow.'

Duncan looked regretful. 'I can't manage tomorrow.'

'Oho!' Pattie made a knowing face. 'With the pretty little fair-haired girl that Gran Brunton mentioned?'

He must have heard about that, or perhaps it was just that he knew who she was talking about, because he laughed and shook his head, and she mimicked Janet's quick embarrassed voice, 'As Janet said, "Oh, *Gran*, that was last *summer*, you know *Duncan*."'

He went on laughing, 'Nice to have friends,' and she said,

'Could I phone you? Because I've had my holiday and I won't really know what my schedule is until I get back into the office on Monday morning.' She felt that she had done very well so far and she mustn't show how much she cared.

Duncan drove her home and she pointed out her window on the first floor. 'That's mine, number three. Will you come up for a coffee or a drink?' She had been going to ramble on 'or anything', but that sounded like an open invitation, and it might not be a good idea to have Duncan too much at home when Michael and Mrs Ames arrived. All the same she was disappointed when he declined, explaining, 'I've got to get back to the exhibition.'

Pattie hated seeing his car go. She had never before felt this urge to race after a car that was pulling away from the kerbside, like the impulse to ask the Bruntons to put her down so that she could run back to Duncan. She thought, I'm hooked. He doesn't know it, and he mustn't know, but that's why pretending to joke about the fair-haired girl was so hard, because it hurts like murder to feel that I'm sharing him.

But she had been lucky. She had come across Duncan without phoning him or obviously chasing him, and he had asked her for a date. She would ring him on Monday, and tonight she would be friendly and welcoming to Michael and his mother.

She had always looked more like Michael's sister than his girl, and that was a relationship she could handle, if she could persuade Michael to settle for it. There never had been very much more. They had said they were in love, their friends had considered them lovers, but with Michael, Pattie had never come across anything like the passion and pain that Duncan aroused in her.

She had small pastries and sandwiches and a quiche for tea, and she stood at the window and saw the taxi arrive on the dot of six. Mrs Ames got out, while Michael paid the taxi and followed her to the front door loaded with shopping. From the number of parcels she had had a good day.

Pattie opened her door and Mrs Ames came at her, offering a cool cheek for a kiss. Usually she bestowed the kiss herself, so this meant that Pattie was out of favour. 'You've been papering, then,' said Mrs Ames, eyeing the living room. 'It's charming. Very nice. And Michael says you did it all on your own.'

Michael certainly hadn't helped. Not that Pattie had wanted him to. He had looked in one evening and then gone off in a huff when a splash of paste landed on his suit.

'Did you get some lovely things?' Pattie asked, but Mrs Ames was not being sidetracked. 'I think so,' she said. 'But I'm dying for some tea,' and no sooner had Pattie poured her a cup than she was enquiring, 'Whatever were you doing in Yorkshire last week, getting yourself snowed up in hunting lodges?'

'I went to interview the man,' Pattie said doggedly, 'but my car crashed and the snow came.'

'And you were up there all alone, just the two of you and nobody else?' Michael had hardly raised the matter again, but his mother was determined to get the facts.

'Nobody,' said Pattie, and Mrs Ames gave a little trill of laughter.

'It's lucky that Michael isn't the jealous type. Some men wouldn't have liked that at all.'

'Don't be ridiculous, Mother,' said Michael, tolerantly testy, and Pattie wondered if he was being big about this because he really considered her above suspicion or because he didn't care that much. She was beginning to learn how savagely real jealousy could lacerate. Duncan and she were hardly more than friends yet, but if they ever did become close she would be primitively possessive. She wouldn't be able to help it. She had no claim on him, but already she hated his other women, whoever they were.

'What was it like in this hunting lodge?' Mrs Ames asked, reaching for a petit four, and Pattie described the big room and knew that she would remember it until her dying day, and went on, 'It was practically a ruin when Duncan first came across it. He rebuilt it, he did a lot of the work himself.' Then she saw from Mrs Ames' expression that there had been too much admiration in her voice, but all the same she added enthusiastically, 'He made a really super job of it.'

'And upstairs?' probed Mrs Ames.

'Two rooms,' said Pattie. She didn't say, 'One bed,' but she looked straight at Michael's mother, who was obviously wondering if Pattie had slept alone. For two pins, thought Pattie, I'd tell you that after Duncan I'm never going to want any other man.

The atmosphere was becoming very highly charged and Michael's head jerked from one woman to the other. His mother hadn't recovered from her initial astonishment at learning that Pattie had spent most of last week all alone with a man whose photographs looked dark and sexy and dangerous, and

Michael could foresee trouble right now. Pattie seemed quite changed from the calm unruffled girl he knew. There was something fiery and defiant about her and he feared that if she spoke the words would be explosive.

He wished profoundly that his mother had not insisted on coming. He never had believed in looking for trouble, and now he was desperately anxious to avert a scene. He began to talk about the weather— would the winter never end? Then he asked what was in the sandwiches and had Pattie watched the late TV movie last night?

He continued the small talk until the moment of confrontation seemed over, while Pattie held back the giggles. Of course it wasn't funny. Mrs Ames was pretty sure that the girl who might have been marrying her son had behaved shamelessly. Michael didn't want to know, but Mrs Ames was going to get to the heart of the matter and it would take more than Michael to stop her.

All through tea he did most of the talking. He was usually on the silent side, but now he worked hard to control the conversation, while every time there was a pause Mrs Ames would clear her throat and hark back to Yorkshire. It seemed she knew the moors well, although from Michael's startled look Pattie was confident that this was the first he had heard of that.

'Where exactly was the hunting lodge?' Mrs Ames asked. Pattie explained, tracing an invisible map with fingertip on the table top, while Mrs Ames nodded, tight-lipped. 'I thought I'd read somewhere that it was right off the beaten track, miles from anywhere. So how did you manage to find it?'

Here came the cross-examination. Michael gave a croak of protest and Pattie said sweetly, 'I was up there last summer.' She felt rather wicked about that, seeing Mrs Ames' open mouth and jabbing finger preparatory to a triumphant, 'Aha, so it wasn't your first visit!' But before Mrs Ames could speak Pattie explained, 'On holiday with some girls from the office. One of them pointed out the lodge as we passed on the road. I remembered where it was.'

'And he wasn't expecting you?'

Pattie shook her head and Michael started to talk about his last summer holiday, and that was how it went on. After tonight Pattie decided she owed it to Michael to tell him she couldn't see him again. She thought he would take it calmly although his mother would be indignant for him, but she couldn't tell him now, and the crazy game continued. Mrs Ames worrying away like a dog with a bone, Michael getting shriller, and Pattie feeling hysterical laughter rising painfully.

She knew now what they meant by 'corpsing' on stage, aching to laugh, so that you had to keep your jaw and your stomach muscles clenched. Most of it had to be nerves, she wasn't enjoying this, but it *was* ridiculous, and if she had dared let herself laugh a little that might have released some of the pressure. For instance, when Mrs Ames pounced on the two paperbacks and opened them, obviously looking for incriminating inscriptions, then pulled a disappointed face, a light laugh might have been in order. But once she started to laugh Pattie wasn't sure how soon she could stop, so she sat silent with shaking shoulders as Mrs Ames replaced the paperbacks on the shelf.

When the ring came on her doorbell Pattie's first thought was, if this is Duncan that will settle everything. But it wasn't Duncan, although it was a man of roughly the same build, big, broad-shouldered, asking if she was Miss Ross.

'Yes,' she said.

'Package for you.' He went clattering down the stairs while she stood in the open doorway, waiting. Behind her, inside the room, she could imagine Mrs Ames craning her neck to see what was going on.

The package was a packing case and it took two men to carry it. Grunting and heaving, they got it up the stairs and Pattie, joined now by Michael, kept staring.

'What is it?' he wanted to know.

She shook her head, looking blank. 'Haven't a clue.'

The two men set down the packing case just inside her door. 'Thank you,' she said. She tipped them and they wished her goodnight, and Mrs Ames asked, 'Weren't you expecting it?'

'Er—no.'

'This is very mysterious. Why didn't you ask them where it came from?'

'Aren't you going to open it?' asked Michael.

She brought the potato peeler to lever off the top that was tacked down. It was the nearest thing she had to a chisel, and although it got bent in the process the lid did lift. Inside was straw and Mrs Ames gave a little squeak.

'It wouldn't be anything alive, would it?'

'How could it breathe, Mother?' Michael pointed out, and Pattie knew that she couldn't hold back the giggles much longer. 'It's a lump of rock,' said

Michael, gingerly scooping out the straw.

'Oh yes,' said Pattie. 'Oh dear!'

'Funny thing for somebody to send you.' He brought out more straw and handed her a note. She knew the writing, she didn't have to look for the signature, although she had known anyway the moment she saw the Cotswold stone. 'This isn't the cat from the exhibition,' Duncan had written, 'you can't have him until the show closes. This is his brother. Try living with him for a few days and see how you get on! Nicely, I'm sure. You have a talent for it.'

She said, 'It's a piece of modern sculpture. If we can get it out you'll see it's a cat as well as a rock.' She couldn't lift it out, not even with Michael's help, and he didn't look inclined to over-exert himself; he was wiping his hands now with a handkerchief. She would have to a borrow a hatchet and hack a way through, but in the meantime she went on scooping out the straw until the carpet was strewn with it and Mrs Ames was coughing from the dust that was rising.

'Who sent it to you?' Michael asked.

'Duncan,' said Pattie, head down in the packing case. 'I saw him at an exhibition this afternoon and I said I liked one like it.'

There was a pregnant silence. She knew what kind of expression was settling on Mrs Ames' face, but she was unprepared for the vigour of her comment. '*Disgusting!*' said Mrs Ames, and Pattie sat back on her heels and blinked. Mrs Ames had the note. She waved it. 'Such bad taste!' she spluttered. 'A talent for living together indeed. You weren't living to- gether, you were snowed in together due to your own stupid fault and the inclement weather. I suppose this is what you'd call an in-joke.' She waved the note again and peered into the packing case and shuddered. 'Revolting object!' she said.

'Oh, I don't know,' said Pattie through quivering lips. 'I rather like rocks, I think they're attractive creatures.'

'A weight like that,' said Mrs Ames, 'could go straight through the floorboards,' and that was the last straw. Pattie started to laugh; and as she had feared, once she started she couldn't stop. Michael had been ready to overlook her days and nights in the hunting lodge, but he couldn't stand her laughter. While Pattie was struggling to restrain herself, but still giggling, he was turning puce. It was Michael who marched out, so fast that Mrs Ames had to collect her parcels herself, while Pattie hiccuped, 'D-don't you want to phone for a taxi?'

'I'm not staying here to be made a fool of,' snapped Michael. 'You seem to have taken leave of your senses. What the hell did that man do to you up there in the cabin?'

That sobered Pattie a little. Last week had changed her, but she hadn't wanted to hurt Michael or anybody. She would have to apologise for laughing, and she called after Mrs Ames, 'I'll ring the taxi rank for you, shall I?

'If it would not be too much trouble,' said Mrs Ames with icy politeness.

After Pattie had rung for the taxi she tried Duncan's number, but got no reply. She could have been with him wherever he was tonight, and she had hoped he might answer, then she could have said, 'Owing to unforeseen circumstances, like the delivery of a rock, my guests left early, so I find myself with a few hours to kill, so what did you have in mind?'

But he hadn't stayed in. She set about sweeping up the straw and packaging it in a dustbin bag. Then she worked on the packing case, levering the tacks with the potato peeler, which took a long time, but at last she got the front panel out and went down on her knees and looked in at her cat. It was very like the one in the exhibition, just that feline hint as thought you had caught it unawares peering out, but the eyes were just as watchful.

She reached in and stroked it. They said Cotswold stone was never cold. She said, 'Will you keep me warm when I'm old, if there's just you and me?' and then bit her lip hard, because that was a bitter thing to say. It came of falling for a man who wasn't in love with you. There were good times ahead, she was sure, but every instinct told her they wouldn't last. 'The crying always ends,' Duncan had said, and so would the laughter one day or night. She would have to go carefully if she didn't want her heart broken.

But she kept on phoning, and she got him just after midnight and wondered if he was alone. 'It's Pattie,' she said. 'It came.'

'That was quick. I said as soon as possible, but they must have got their skates on.'

'Thank you. I'm going to enjoy living with it, although the note gave Michael's mother a fit. She thinks it was very bad form for you to refer to "living together" after last week. Disgusting, in fact.'

'Funny woman,' he said. 'What did you tell them about last week?'

'Nothing.'

'And does "living together" sound disgusting to

you?' She could hear him smiling. The words, 'Come live with me and be my love and we will all the pleasures prove . . .' sang a siren song in her head, and she said, 'No.'

'We must discuss it some time.' He sounded as if he was still smiling and this was too fast, and when he asked, 'May I come round?' Pattie said, 'It's late, can I see you Monday evening?'

'All right.'

Oh, you fool, she thought, as she put the phone down, what are you scared about? But she knew that she was afraid of loving and losing . . .

Sunday passed without incident. Pattie lazed about in her apartment, reading the Sunday papers and Duncan's paperbacks. They were powerful books, both of them, making her realise again how little she really knew of this man. She was starved for him, as though his touch was food and drink to her, but she hardly knew him at all.

Nothing much happened to Pattie on Sunday, but Monday made up for it. As soon as she got into the office she was greeted with a barrage of knowing smiles. 'No need to ask you if you enjoyed your holiday,' said Miss Grey, head of the library department, travelling up in the lift with her. 'When you came in for his cuttings I never thought this was what it would lead to.' Miss Grey didn't sound entirely approving, but although she shook her neatly coiffured grey head at Pattie her eyes were twinkling, and all Pattie could do was blush.

Roz Rickard, the features editor who had sent Pattie after Duncan in the first place, looked like the cat with the cream, grinning from ear to ear. 'Who's your fairy godmother, then?' she said as Pattie walked across to her desk. 'Who couldn't stand them rough and tough and sexy?'

Roz had spoken to Pattie on the phone a couple of times since Pattie got back from Yorkshire, but Pattie hadn't told her how she felt about Duncan, nor admitted that her stay in the lodge had been anything but platonic. Now she laughed, 'He does have a way with him. You could get to like him,' and Roz hooted,

'And there's the picture to prove it.'

'What picture?'

She hadn't opened her newspaper. She had picked it up on her way out, her mind full of personal matters. 'Not Willie's page again?' she groaned. But there she was. 'After last week's ordeal when they were marooned in an isolated hunting lodge on the Yorkshire moors author/TV personality Duncan Keld and reporter Pattie Ross got together again on Saturday at an exhibition of rock sculpture,' said the caption. 'Shortly afterwards they left. Together, of course.'

Nobody had bothered to get a quote from them, and it hadn't been necessary because the picture spoke for itself. Duncan was a dark figure looking down, but it was the moment when he put his hand on Pattie's and joy had flooded over her. It seemed to her now that even in the smudged newspaper print her heart was in her eyes for anyone to see, and she said huskily, 'How could they?' But of course they could, she had worked in this line of journalism herself.

'It's a lovely picture,' Roz enthused. 'You look terrific.' Pattie nodded, forcing a smile, and Roz was suddenly aware of her vulnerability. The picture was happy, but the girl was open to hurt, the dark man gave nothing away. Roz suspected he could be a ruthless bastard, and she said quietly, 'Play it cool, eh? Don't go tossing your bonnet over any windmills.'

'Oh no,' said Pattie, 'I won't be doing that,' and she only wished she could believe herself.

There was a lot of teasing that day, because everybody had seen the photograph. Pattie had thought Duncan might phone about it, but he didn't, and anyway she was seeing him tonight. She sketched out her article on him. If this could have appeared promptly the gossip would have been good publicity, but by the time it reached the news-stands nobody would remember that Pattie Ross had been snowed in with Duncan.

She would have to start from scratch, explaining how she had gone seeking a story, with him angered at first by her unscheduled arrival but afterwards accepting the inevitable. When her readers were reading this she and Duncan might still be seeing each other, or they might have gone their separate ways, and she felt that it would be tempting fate to even hint how close they had been for those few days, so she wrote in a light vein with the chimney fire as the big scene. She could say that she wasn't exactly thrilled when the snowplough got through, but she couldn't say that Duncan was coming for her tonight, and the thought of being alone with him again made her ache with a longing that blotted everything else from her mind.

He was taking her out to dinner, but she would rather have stayed at home with him, so at lunchtime she bought steaks. When he came, unless he had booked, she could suggest that she laid on the meal. In any case she had a super new tangerine silk dress with a wide black suede belt to show off her slim waist, and if they did go out she had blown a hole in her bank balance with a black velvet full-length trench coat. She had gone to the exhibition in a suit and her camel coat, but she was putting on the glamour tonight.

Her apartment was five minutes away from the tube if you walked quickly, which she did. It was still very cold and she had things to do in the hour and a half before Duncan came. She didn't give the car standing outside the house more than a glance, she didn't know it, but as she walked the short flagged path from the gate to the front door she heard footsteps behind her. A girl, in a grey fox coat and hat, called as she turned, 'Is it Pattie Ross?'

'Yes. Do I——'

'I'm Jennifer Stanley.' Pattie had only seen Jennifer Stanley in photographs, but now she recognised her, and she was breathtaking. 'Please, I want to talk to you,' said Jennifer. 'It won't take long, but it is rather important.'

'What about?' Pattie still had a conscience about the gossip item that had caused the wedding to be cancelled, but Jennifer smiled,

'Oh, I know you were the reporter who found out about Duncan and me, but I don't bear you any grudges for that. I'd like us to be friends.'

'*Friends?*' Pattie echoed. She couldn't understand this, but she led the way upstairs and opened her door. She skirted the packing case and dumped her shopping bag and said, 'Do sit down.'

Jennifer seated herself on the settee, carefully arranging her coat around her. The furs were fabulous, the hat framed the heart-shaped face, pretty as a picture. 'I've got a lot to thank you for,' said Jennifer Stanley earnestly. 'I might have married a man who didn't really love me.'

'I suppose you might,' Pattie agreed because Jennifer seemed to be waiting for her to say something. When she did Jennifer smiled, 'Instead of dear Wilfred who loves me very, very much. I'm very happy.'

'I'm glad,' said Pattie, which she was, although it seemed strange that Jennifer Stanley should go to the trouble of coming here to tell her this.

'In a way I owe it to you for the way things have turned out for me,' Jennifer went on, 'so I want to help you too. I saw your picture in this morning's paper and I thought—oh, the poor girl! Because, you see, I know how it's going to end, I know what Duncan could do to you. What I rather think he might be planning to do.'

'You're not making much sense,' said Pattie.

'I'm sorry,' Jennifer made a charming little gesture of helplessness, 'but I do want you to understand. It was so awful when Nigel jilted me at the last minute like that. I just went to pieces, I'm not a very strong character.' In the luxurious furs she looked tiny and fragile, and when she closed her eyes her lashes made long dark shadows on her pale cheeks. 'I—tried to kill myself,' she said huskily, and Pattie gasped in horror.

'I didn't know.'

'Hardly anyone knew. Duncan knew, though. He was very upset, very angry.'

'I can imagine,' said Pattie, and Jennifer's eyes flew open.

'I don't think you can imagine how much he hated you.'

Pattie winced and heard herself protesting, 'That wasn't fair! Why put all the blame on me? He was as much to blame himself. Nigel was as much to blame.' And so, of course, was Jennifer.

'But I'm not blaming you,' said Jennifer in a soft rush of words. 'Not at all, that's what I'm telling you. But Duncan's taken up with you now and he'll hurt you in the end. He'll reject you.'

Pattie knew that he would tire of her because he did not love her, but surely he would never reject her for the savage satisfaction of revenge. 'Did he sleep with you up at the lodge?' asked Jennifer, and Pattie's betraying blush answered her, and she said, 'He's a wonderful lover, isn't he?' as though they were discussing his writing or his skill as an after-dinner speaker, and Pattie felt sick.

'Duncan never takes his women seriously,' said Jennifer. 'He'd never put one of them before his work for a minute. I'm sure you found that out up at the lodge, and right now I'm sure he's fond of you.' She stood up and stroked the fur of her coat with little grey-kid hands. 'But deep down,' she said, 'there's all this anger, and as soon as the novelty wears off he's going to dump you quite brutally, and I don't think you deserve that, so I think you should be warned.'

'Thank you,' said Pattie. As Jennifer walked towards the door she added, 'But don't worry about me,' and Jennifer shook her head.

'Poor Pattie,' she said. 'Poor, poor Pattie.'

CHAPTER EIGHT

IT was a long time before Pattie could stop shivering. She couldn't believe it was gratitude that had brought Jennifer Stanley here, but if things had been as bad as that for her last year Duncan might still have this rankling resentment against Pattie. She wondered if Jennifer had been the pretty little fair-haired girl up at the lodge last summer, and the pictures that came into her mind corroded her with jealousy.

Jennifer knew all about Duncan as a lover, she knew that he didn't take his affairs seriously. But for Pattie the affair was serious already. If she let it get a tighter hold it would take over her life. Right now Duncan had temporarily forgotten that a girl had tried to kill herself because of something Pattie had written, but Pattie could never be more than a passing fancy for him because deep down he did not like her, so the foundations of any relationship would be rotten.

I wish he wasn't coming tonight, she thought. I wish I hadn't gone looking for him, because sure enough he would never have come searching for me.

She might have phoned even at this late stage, and pleaded a headache or a last-minute business appointment, but she convinced herself that wasn't a good idea. Why make such a fuss? So long as she kept her cool and got in no deeper, there was no reason why she shouldn't enjoy Duncan's company.

She had never taken such care, getting ready for a date. She slipped into the new dress and dabbed on a new perfume. This one was sharper than the perfume Michael bought for her, that she had always thought was her favourite. She had changed and if Duncan had loved her she would have really blossomed, but he didn't and he wouldn't. Jennifer had made her see that. It had been bad enough when her father never came back, but she could become so dependent on Duncan that losing him would finish her. So she must watch her every word and every move, and keep the relationship casual and easy.

She was standing at the window when his car drew up in a space across the road, and the pull that drew her towards him was so strong that she looked around for something to hold on to. She wanted to run downstairs and be at the front door before he reached it. But she stood by the sideboard, gripping the edge, until the ring came on her own bell, and then she called, 'Come in.'

He was immaculately dressed, in a dark suit and a dark coat, grey shirt and tie. Pattie said, 'Hi,' as he came towards her, and his smile made her catch her breath, and when he kissed her she felt herself go spiralling down and down. All she wanted to do was stop fighting and stop thinking, but that was the way to so much pain and anyway the kiss was light, just a 'Hello' greeting.

As he loosed her she said, 'Could you help me get a cat out of a box?'

They scooped out more straw, Duncan broke down more of the packing case, and finally dragged the rock cat clear and asked, 'Where do you want him?'

'There isn't a fireplace, he'd have looked good by

a fire. In the corner maybe.'

Pushing and shoving left a deep trail across the carpet. 'He weighs a ton,' said Duncan.

'Michael's mother was worried about the floor-boards.'

'Michael's mother could have a point.'

The crouching cat's eyes seemed to follow Pattie as she moved. She said, 'He does watch you, doesn't he?'

'That's the idea.' Duncan began gathering up straw and tossing it back into the packing case, his grin quick and infectious. 'If I'm not watching you something is,' he said, and she laughed.

'Now what do you imagine I could be up to?'

'Looking like that,' he said, 'there are no limits,' joking because he wouldn't really care. She sat down beside the stone cat, stroking its head, and thought how splendid it would have looked up at the lodge, in the big inglenook fireplace with the log fire crackling.

She said, 'Michael and his mother were here when he arrived.' She picked up a few pieces of straw that had been trailed right across the carpet. 'It was the last straw,' she said.

'Oh?' He waited to hear how and she grimaced, 'I started to giggle. I'd had a hard time not laughing before because Mrs Ames kept asking questions and Michael was rabbiting about everything under the sun to try to shut her up. She thought it was very stupid of me to get myself snowed in with somebody like you.'

Duncan's grin was slow this time, and the devilish gleam was in his eyes. 'Not a fan?' he said.

'Oh no.'

'Did Michael think it was stupid?'

'Oh yes.' She shrugged. 'But he didn't really want to know. He'd have turned a blind eye and a deaf ear until I started to laugh, then he came the nearest to blowing his top I've ever seen him.'

'Was it an eye-opener?' The light was still dancing in Duncan's dark eyes.

'Not very dramatic,' she said. 'He turned pale purple and spluttered. And left his mother to carry her own parcels.'

Duncan feigned astonishment, 'The big gesture!' Then he changed the subject. 'You saw the photograph this morning, in that bloody column?'

'Mmm.' So would Michael and Mrs. Ames.

'At least it was a good one of you.' He didn't sound as though she had made a fool of herself looking like an adoring teenager, so perhaps it wasn't as bad as she thought. She had known how she felt, but the people who had teased her today had only said she looked happy, not in love. Happiness was all right.

She probably wasn't in love, but she was almost overwhelmingly attracted to him. If they stayed here much longer he would surely kiss her again, properly this time, and she would go up in flames. 'Shall we go?' she said. She hurried to wash her hands from the dust of the rock and get into her coat. Duncan looked around the room as he waited for her. 'It smells new,' he said. 'What have you been doing?'

'I papered those walls, and gave the others a fresh coat of paint.' There were closed doors, into the kitchenette and her bedroom, and if she showed him round the small apartment she would have to open the bedroom door. She daren't do that because what she really wanted was for Duncan to pick her up and càrry her to the bed. 'I'm starving,' she said, 'I'm really starving. Where are we going to have our dinner?'

He took her to a restaurant that was new to her. Outside it didn't look much, but inside lamps glowed and a woman came to meet them with a smile as warm as the lamplight. She was middle-aged, with fair hair plaited around her head, wearing a long bibbed apron over her dress. She spoke in a language Pattie didn't recognise while a man, heavily built with heavy features, gave Duncan a welcoming bear-hug. Old friends, thought Pattie, as they were guided to their table and Duncan was hailed by several of the other diners.

They were taken down into the cellars to select the wine. The cellars seemed bigger than the restaurant, racks and racks of bottles, some of them thick-coated with dust. Joe, the proprietor, and Duncan walked ahead of Pattie between the rows discussing vintages, sometimes in English, sometimes in what was probably Joe's native tongue. Duncan seemed as fluent as Joe, and afterwards at the table Pattie asked, 'How many languages can you speak?'

'A few,' said Duncan.

'That wasn't mentioned in the articles I've read about you.'

'I don't think anybody ever asked me before.' He poured wine for her. 'But if you roam around as much as I do you're bound to pick up another language or two eventually.'

Joe and his wife hovered, providing impeccable service for a valued guest. 'Where did you meet them?' Pattie asked.

'In Hungary,' said Duncan, and she thought, I

could have such adventures with you. Your life is so full and exciting. But you're never going to ask me to share it, except perhaps for a little while, then it would be a goodbye that would hurt more than death.

She hadn't told him that Jennifer had been waiting for her when she returned from the office, but warmed and encouraged by the wine, she began, 'Jennifer Stanley——' and Duncan said curtly, 'I'd prefer not to discuss Jennifer.'

A moment before he had been smiling, but at the mention of Jennifer's name he was suddenly un-approachable, and she thought, it's true, he still blames me for that newspaper story. Deep down, like Jennifer said, there is still the anger.

Then he leaned across and ran his fingers down her arm, and it was like a trail of fire to her so that she had to hold back a cry. There was still the anger, but overlying it was this tremendous charge of sexuality. She watched his fingers, long and strong, wrists showing brown against the pale grey cuffs of his shirt, and she wanted to reach for his hands and press them hard to her fast beating heart. She was aching for him.

Then he smiled again. Forget Jennifer, his smile said, let's just enjoy the meal and the moment and later ourselves. So she ate and drank and smiled too, and talked quite a lot, and when most of the tables cleared Joe and his wife joined them over coffee and brandy and there was more talk and laughter.

Pattie was sorry when their evening here ended and she and Duncan drove away. She was tinglingly aware of him sitting close beside her, the movements of his driving. When they reached her home and he took her in his arms how was she going to hold him away while every nerve in her was crying for him? But how could she let him make love to her when all it would mean to him was satisfying an appetite? I'd be like another piece of Stilton, she thought wryly, or a good cigar.

He would expect to be invited in to stay a while, because he found her desirable and he knew that she wanted him. She only hoped he didn't suspect how badly. His attraction for her was almost irresistible but not quite. The night was not going to end with her lying in Duncan's arms, but she was not at all sure how she was going to avert that.

She might try, 'I've got a busy day tomorrow and it's late.' She could hardly say, 'No, because you fancy me but you don't like me, while I could go crazy for you. I could run whimpering after you next time you go aroaming to the other side of the world and you wouldn't like that, would you? and neither would I.'

She said, 'This isn't the road,' suddenly realising he was driving her the wrong way home.

'I thought you might like to see my place,' he said, and she hesitated.

'It's late, but—yes, all right.'

She would like to see how he lived in London, compare it with the lodge. He looked a different man in town, suave, sophisticated, tough, still, but there wasn't much sign of Heathcliff's roughness.

His apartment was the top floor and attics of a large converted Victorian house overlooking one of the parks. The main room was vast, and warm although no fire burned in the Adam fireplace. In daytime light would stream through the three tall windows with their pointed tops, and there were ceiling lights, but now the room was shadowy with diffused lighting.

Books lined almost the whole of one wall. On the other walls were pictures, modern ones, some bright in barbaric colours, some of intricate workmanship. There was a lot to see in this room. One of the rock carvings sat on a low shelf. Pattie crossed to it and it seemed to be just rock—about a third the size of her cat—then she saw the eyes, sleepy, drowsing in the sun.

The furniture was mostly modern, big comfortable chairs, pieces in beautiful gleaming wood. Duncan might have brought some of these things back with him from his travels, the Spanish rugs, the Aztec figurines. It was luxurious, and interesting, and when he asked, 'What's the matter?' she blinked,

'Nothing—you've got quite a place here.'

'Then why are you frowning?'

She hadn't realised she was, then she realised why and said slowly, 'I suppose I was thinking how different it is from the lodge. The lodge is stark. You don't have any furniture at all in the big upstairs room. Why don't you take some of this up there?'

'Because I like the lodge how it is,' he said, and after a moment Pattie agreed, 'Yes,' and smiled, 'It wouldn't do, would it?'

The lodge was his escape. He wasn't a rich man there, but because he was strong and self-sufficient he was at home in the loneliness and the wildness of the moors. So could I be, she thought, if you would take me back; but you couldn't get rid of me fast enough when the snowplough got through. I might get invited to the lodge in summertime, when your friends drift up there. But not when you go alone because nobody is welcome then, and come summer we might not even be friends.

Gently he turned her towards him and she thought, this is all there is for him. He wants me physically, and God knows she wanted him too. When he started to kiss her she could have clung to him like a drowner to a rescuer. It was that hard to pull back. It was like letting go of life, but she held her arms tight to her sides, fists clenched. 'No,' she said through gritted teeth. '*No!*'

'All right.' He let her go. 'Now what the hell is the matter?'

'I don't want to stay here tonight, if that was what you were thinking.' He gave a small rueful nod, and she gabbled on, 'It's too fast for me. I don't rush into affairs, not even brief affairs. Up at the lodge things were sort of mixed up and crazy, but this is real life here and I'm used to sleeping in my own bed and I want to go home, please, now.'

'You won't even stay for a drink?'

She had had enough. Very little more could melt her resistance so that she couldn't think of next week or next month, only of tonight and the agonising sweetness of dark hours with Duncan.

'No, thank you,' she said, sounding like a prim child.

'Not even if I promise to take you home afterwards, untouched?' He was laughing at her. To his mind she must seem both prudish and ridiculous, and she said wretchedly,

'I'm sorry. It was a lovely meal, a lovely evening, but I've had enough to drink and I would like to go home.'

'Then you shall.' He drove her back to her apartment. Neither said much, but when the car stopped he asked, 'Can I see you tomorrow?' and Pattie blurted, 'Oh *yes*!'

She had been terrified he wouldn't ask. He didn't kiss her goodnight, but he got out of the car and walked with her to the door, and as her key turned and the door swung in he said quietly, 'I wish you'd stayed.'

He went then and Pattie climbed the stairs to her empty flat. If she had stayed she would have been wrapped in his arms now. She remembered how warm it had been, how comforting, and she felt so lonely that she went across to the rock cat, sat down on the floor and put a hand on it. 'Will you keep me warm when I'm old, if there's just the two of us?' she had said earlier, and tonight she felt old. And a fool, sitting here stroking a rock for company.

Perhaps she was crazy not to take what was offered, and let tomorrow look after itself. She had come near. If Duncan hadn't stopped kissing her she would have started to kiss him. If he had been less amenable about bringing her home the moment she asked she could have ended up spending the night in his bed.

Which showed he wasn't all that bothered. Oh, he wanted her, but with his sex appeal there would always be other girls. Just as there would always be the shadow of Jennifer Stanley falling between them. Pattie had shown some sense, some control. If she had stayed she would have regretted it by morning. But that didn't stop her crying into her pillow as though her heart was breaking . . .

I won't see him again, she decided, gulping her first cup of coffee. She longed and longed for him, but once she gave way again she would never know another moment's peace. She would do whatever he wanted, go wherever he went. She would be caught like a moth in a flame. So she would finish it now before the flame consumed her.

She rang his number at once before she changed her mind and after a while he answered, sounding as though he was yawning. 'It's Pattie,' she said. 'About tonight. I'm sorry, but I can't make it after all, I've got to work late.'

'How late?' he said. 'Doing what?'

Stupidly she hadn't got her answer ready, and she stammered, launching into a rambling account of having to meet a much-married actress who was passing through London and leaving early in the morning. She had forgotten about that last night, but now she remembered, and on Wednesday she had to go away herself.

'Don't be silly,' said Duncan. 'I'll be at your place at half past seven. If you're not there I'll wait.'

She panicked a little that day. It wasn't so much that Duncan was closing in on her as the force of her own longings that frightened her. Roz had warned her to keep her cool, but if she had told Roz, 'I want him so badly that it hurts all the time,' Roz would probably have said, 'Then have him, for goodness' sake—he fancies you, doesn't he?' 'But it won't last, will it?' 'Oh no.' Roz knew that, everybody knew that. The advice most of them would give her would be to have a fling if she wanted, a raging affair if she was mad for the man. Take what she wanted and pay for it. But nobody would offer any hope that it was going to last.

So she told no one how she felt. She got through

her work and a typical office day, and when she came back to the flat she put through a call to her mother. They phoned each other often and wrote regularly. Pattie's stepfather was a nice man, her mother was lucky in husbands. Both had been kind, and proud of her pretty youthful looks. Pattie had visited her mother's house and been welcomed and assured by her stepfather that she could make a home with them any time she wished.

She was wondering now if she might do that for a while. She liked her job, but she could freelance, and a change of everything might be the answer when she no longer had Duncan. If she had a fresh start planned at least there would be somewhere to run.

Her mother had just received Pattie's letter, written in the lodge, but Pattie hadn't mentioned the lodge, and now she said, 'I was snowed up in Yorkshire a few days ago.'

'Oh, Yorkshire's so pretty,' said her mother.

It hadn't been pretty. It had been terrible and beautiful. 'There was a man,' Pattie began.

'Michael?' said her mother. 'I must say, I do like the sound of Michael.' She gave a delicate little sniff and began to talk about a troublesome head cold that was making her look an absolute sight. 'It's the storms from Alaska,' she explained. 'They're so cold and quite wild,' and Pattie realised that nothing here would matter as much to her mother as the red nose she was dabbing now with a soft handkerchief.

Her mother was the child. She couldn't take problems to her mother, much less heartbreak. Whatever happened to her she would have to fight for her own survival. So nothing was going to happen. Nothing more than friendship.

They hadn't discussed what they were doing tonight, so she changed into a lighter dress and wondered whether she should be providing a meal. Yesterday's steaks were still in the fridge, but she was apprehensive about staying in, just the two of them, and she checked the What's On columns for films.

The street door was closed tonight. She saw Duncan walking from where he had parked his car, and she went down and opened the door and said, 'Hello,' then walked a little ahead of him back up here. She began to talk. 'Are we doing anything in particular? I mean, you just said you'd be around. I didn't know how to dress, I didn't know what we'd be doing.'

'But you know one thing we won't be doing,' said Duncan.

Pattie turned, half way across the room, and he was laughing and she said, 'That's right.'

Suddenly he looked serious. 'I agree, what happened at the lodge doesn't count here. That was an exceptional situation and you were in a state of stress.'

He meant that she was hysterical. He must think she was an excitable nervous type, which wasn't true. 'No,' she said, 'It doesn't count.' But she would never forget a minute of it. Then he smiled again and his nearness pierced her to the heart.

'Personally,' he said, 'I enjoyed our time together immensely, after the first two days. But I promise you, no passes. Of course if you should care to make a move I'll be here. Well, for the next two weeks.'

He was amused by her Puritan stand but not involved enough to do anything about it. Perhaps he thought she would come round to him. His record must have taught him all the tricks, including the waiting game, and it was really no compliment to be guaranteed hands-off. She heard herself say, 'Two weeks?'

'I'm off to New Zealand in a fortnight.'

So she didn't have to run away because he was going. She could surely get through two weeks without making a fool of herself, and she took a deep breath and managed a smile. 'Don't you get around? Where are we going tonight? There's a film.'

'There's a party,' he said.

It was a very good party, given by one of his television colleagues to celebrate the sale of a TV series to America. There were well-known faces mingling with unknowns, but although everybody looked successful and most of them attractive, Duncan dominated the scene. Physically he was taller and bigger than most of the men, and he had a charisma that meant he was never on the fringe, always in the centre of any group he joined. People made way for him, looked at him and listened to him. But more than once she felt the black churning jealousy when some girl or other touched and flirted. She had no rights of course, no claim, so she tried to ignore and pretend not to notice.

She knew some of the guests, and the ones who didn't know her knew her magazine and accepted her as part of the show-biz scene. She and Duncan stayed together all evening and she sensed the sidewards glances as she was assessed, and once she heard someone say, 'She's pretty enough but not up to his usual standard,' and she was sure they were talking about her.

He drove her back home. On the way they discussed

folk who had been at the party, and he kept her smiling, and when they reached her flat he said goodbye to her and asked, 'All right for tomorrow night?'

'Yes, I suppose.'

'Goodnight, then.' Pattie watched the car draw away, the memory of a final smile and wave with her, and reflected that he hadn't given her a chance to say, 'Coming up for a coffee?' or even to lift her face to be kissed. He was sticking to his part of the bargain, offering nothing unless she asked, and that suited her because she couldn't compete with his usual run of girl-friends and she would be out of her mind to try.

She saw a lot of Duncan in the following days. Everybody took it for granted that they had an affair going. Pattie was teased and envied, and she loved going around with him. He had so much energy, such a talent for brightening the greyest day. She spent almost all her free time with him, he liked her company, there was no doubt of that, and it was like being young all over again.

Not that she was old, at twenty-two for heaven's sake, but after her father died she had never been without care. She had had her mother to worry about, then her career, shouldering every responsibility herself. She had never again felt young-at-heart but she did with Duncan. When he collected her from work, which he did most evenings, she felt as light as a gas-filled balloon, as though she could go sailing over the rooftops unless somebody grabbed hold of her and held her down. Duncan didn't grab her, but she always slipped her hand through his arm and that kept her feet on the ground.

Some nights he took her to fabulous restaurants, other nights they had hamburgers and chips. They went around with his friends—he knew everybody, she decided. They mixed with crowds. Sometimes they stayed in his apartment and listened to music and talked like old friends, but even then he took her home when she glanced at her fob watch, which was usually around midnight. Not once did he even kiss her.

It wasn't all that long, of course. Just a week and a half, and when she was in her own bed, alone, she spent sleepless hours wondering if Duncan had decided to leave things the way she had said she wanted them. To give sex a miss, which was probably a novelty for him. She was probably his first platonic girl-friend, but there would always be plenty of the others around. Or if he believed that before he went she would capitulate of her own free will. Say 'I'll stay tonight,' or flirt like the girls she saw eyeing him, getting a blatant message across.

She didn't think she could do that, because surely if he had really wanted her he would have taken her by now. He hardly touched her. He treated her as though they had been friends for years. I could be his *sister*, she thought. He gives me a wonderful time, when I'm with him it's fantastic. It's the nights when I'm alone that I know how much more I want.

But then she remembered Jennifer, and what they were telling her already—that her 'affair' with Duncan Keld wouldn't last—and this was safer, and better, she supposed. He could brighten a grey day, but losing him would blacken the sun, and if she was going to miss him that much as a friend how would it be if she had been losing a lover?

She marked off the days in her mind. Not on a calendar, she would have hated to literally cross them out, as though they were finished and done with, but as each day ended she thought, one day nearer goodbye. And as it came close she knew that Duncan had taken her at her word and was going to keep his.

They spent their last evening together in Joe's restaurant and she was trying to forget that after tonight it would be months before she saw him again. She was especially gay, putting on a brave face because she mustn't let anyone see how miserable she felt.

She had had enough sympathy that day. It was common knowledge that Duncan was going away. 'What a shame!' everybody in the office kept saying, and she had had a phone call from Clare, for the gossip page, asking how she felt about it.

'It's a small world,' Pattie had said, and Clare had retorted, 'Not that small,' adding, 'Will you be waiting for him when he comes back?'

I hope not, Pattie thought, but I think I might be waiting for the rest of my life. She said, 'Of course, it's always nice to see friends again, and although I know it sounds corny that's all we are, good friends.'

It was all they were. It was just bad luck that Pattie was obsessed by him. She told him about the phone call and he said, 'They must be short of copy. By the way, I've got some news for you.' For a moment she wondered if he wasn't going after all, but he said, 'About your car. They've finally got it to a garage.'

'The poor old thing! What's the verdict?'

'Barney said he had hopes for it, I'll give you their number.' Pattie wrote down the phone number of the Bruntons' farm in her little notebook, and resolved to ring tomorrow and thank them for going to the trouble of hauling her car out of the gorge. The weather was still bad up there, it couldn't have been easy.

If I go up to collect it, she thought, I could drive back to the lodge. But I wouldn't be able to get in and Duncan wouldn't be there, it would just be empty and cold. From tonight Duncan wouldn't be here either and every day was going to be empty and cold, and he asked, 'Are you all right?'

'Yes, of course.'

'You look tired.'

'Well, it's getting late, isn't it?' She could have bitten her tongue then because she didn't want the evening to end; and it didn't. There was quite a crowd in Joe's tonight and most of them stayed on, giving Duncan a send-off, so that Pattie's eyes were heavy-lidded by the time Duncan drove her home.

Outside her house he said, 'Goodbye, love.'

'Goodbye.' There had been no suggestion of her meeting him tomorrow, which would be his last day and on which he had business appointments, or seeing him off at the airport.

He reached across and opened her door, and the cold air came in and she knew that he wasn't going to take her in his arms even now. He was smiling at her. 'It's been nice knowing you,' he said.

'Yes.' She nodded stiffly, like a puppet. 'It's been super. I shall miss you.' She got out of the car and he didn't stop her or follow her. The car engine was still running. 'I'll be home tomorrow evening,' he said. 'Any time after eight. Come round if you feel like it,' and the car slipped smoothly into gear and roared away into the night, leaving her shaking.

Until now she had thought she had no part in tomorrow, that tonight was her goodbye, but now he was suggesting she went to him tomorrow night. He wouldn't come for her, but if she chose she could knock on his door or ring his bell. Pacing her room, she talked to the rock cat. 'It's all up to me, isn't it? He could have made it easier for me, he only had to reach out, any time. I couldn't have held him off again, and he must have know that. This has been a sort of seduction, keeping everything platonic, hardly touching me, because I want him now more desperately than ever, and I shall go tomorrow night, of course I shall, but he could have made it easier.'

She knew she was a fool. One night and then he would catch his plane, and by the time he returned he would probably have forgotten Pattie Moss. Or near enough. But she wouldn't forget Duncan Keld because he was in her blood, part of her. She had hardly given Michael a thought since he stalked out of her flat, and yet at one time she had imagined she loved Michael. She knew different now, and it was ironic that Michael should phone next morning . . .

He hadn't been in touch, but he chose today, having read in the gossip column that Duncan Keld was leaving England, researching another book, and that Pattie had insisted they were just good friends. Michael knew that Duncan and Pattie had been around together, but he had missed Pattie and he was prepared to start up again. Not on the old terms at once, of course, but a meeting might show if they had any hopes of eventually getting back on the old familiar footing.

He said, 'I see your friend from the hunting lodge is leaving the country. That should leave you with some free time. What are you going to do now?'

Pattie remembered an ancient film she had seen, probably on TV, where an old woman, whose lover had died or gone years before, was asked what happened afterwards, and who had turned empty despairing eyes on her questioner and replied, 'There was no afterwards.'

Pattie felt a little the same way herself, as though a black wall blocked out all her tomorrows, but she said brightly, 'Oh, I'll think of something. Sorry, I don't have time to talk, but I've got a hundred things to do right now,' and added with a touch of mischief, 'Remember me to your mother,' before she put down the office phone.

She hadn't told anyone she would be seeing Duncan tonight. She was quite busy and she kept fairly cheerful in front of them all. So Duncan was off, she had never expected him to stay. He would be phoning, writing, and so would she, and it wasn't all that big a world these days. Roz suggested that Pattie came home with her for dinner and she felt a hypocrite declining, pretending she had already fixed to meet another friend.

Nobody knew she was going to Duncan. There was no reason why they shouldn't, it wasn't a secret, but she couldn't talk about it and she couldn't have said whether the prospect filled her with joy or despair. She was going because she couldn't keep away, but he could keep away from her. He had shown that every night since they met again. It would be a kind of defeat for her, turning up, because she knew and he knew that if she did she would stay till morning.

She packed a toothbrush in her handbag, and some

small cosmetic items. If there should be other folk around, and she had made a mistake and Duncan did intend to bring her back, an overnight bag would have been dreadfully embarrassing. She had booked a taxi, and in the ten minutes or so before it was due to arrive she rang the Bruntons.

Janet answered and Pattie said, 'I've been meaning to get in touch,' that was true, she had, 'To thank you for everything, and now Duncan tells me you've got my car up. I do appreciate that.'

Janet gave her the garage run-down on the car repairs, which all things considering didn't sound too bad, and then she said, 'Oh, we found your medallion. The chain's broken, but apart from that it's OK.'

'Oh, *marvellous*!'

'We posted it to Duncan a couple of days ago.' He might have received it this morning, if not surely it would arrive tomorrow. Pattie said again how grateful she was and Janet asked 'How are you and Duncan getting on?'

'Fine,' said Pattie. 'But he's off to New Zealand tomorrow, so this is our last evening,' and Janet said, as if she sympathised,

'Yes, well, that's Duncan, he never stays in one place long. Give him our love, won't you?'

'I will,' Pattie promised. Their love and hers. Only theirs was friendship and hers was passion and longing, but anyway she now had a good excuse for arriving at his apartment. She had come for her talisman.

She rang his bell and he answered. Her heart lurched when she saw him and she thought, it will always be like this. He will always be able to set my pulses racing as though a fever has hit me. She gabbled breathlessly, 'I phoned Janet Brunton and she said they'd found my charm and she posted it to you a couple of days ago—has it come yet?'

'Sorry.'

'Oh dear,' she said. 'Wouldn't it be the limit if it got lost in the post?' They were walking up the staircase to Duncan's apartment. She couldn't hear any sound from up there, so perhaps there was no one else, and she was glad. She didn't think she could have gone on putting on a brave face, talking small talk.

As they came through the door, into the big empty room, he asked, 'Was that all you came for?' and she said simply, 'I was coming anyway.'

'Know something?' She heard him starting to smile. She hadn't looked straight at him till then, but now she did, and he said, 'We could have passed on the way, I was coming to you.' Pattie took the two steps between them and his arms went round her. She was scared she was going to burst into tears. She pressed her face into his shoulder and she was shaking like a leaf and he said quietly, 'It's all right now. It's always going to be all right.'

No, not always. Not from tomorrow. But while she was in his arms it was so right that nothing else mattered. 'I don't care,' she said, 'I can't let you go without telling you I love you. Without showing you I do. I'm sorry about Jennifer Stanley.'

'What's she got to do with it?' He sounded as though Jennifer Stanley had no place in this conversation, and Pattie certainly didn't want to talk about her, but she had to explain,

'Well, she came round to my flat. She said she

didn't hold any grudge against me because she was marrying a man who really loved her now, but that you blamed me still.'

Duncan swore, briefly but vividly. Then he said, 'I felt guilty enough about Jennifer myself. I took it out on you, but I blamed myself.'

'Did she——' Pattie's voice had a hushed horror, 'did she try to kill herself?'

'She did take an overdose, but she knew she was going to be found in time. I saw quite a lot of her last summer, I felt responsible for her.'

That was a story the gossip hounds had missed. It was going to hurt, but she had to ask, 'Were you lovers last summer?' and when he said, 'No,' she knew he was telling the truth. 'But I *was* sorry for her,' he went on. 'I still am, although she's a greedy woman. Being jilted like that was a savage blow to her pride, but it was losing a rich man that really cut her up. The man she is marrying isn't going to provide such a cushy life style.'

So that was why she came round to poison my mind, Pattie thought with a flash of perception. Telling me you hated me still. She was the one who hated me. She wanted to keep us apart as her little revenge.

She said slowly, 'She said you'd never really forgiven me for that story. That when you finished fancying me you'd get rid of me so fast.'

'My darling idiot,' said Duncan, 'I don't fancy you.'

'You don't?'

His arms were still around her, not holding her crushingly close any more but she was still within the circle of them, and he wasn't joking, there was no smile in his dark eyes. 'I'm burned up for you,' he said huskily. 'You rip the heart out of me every time I look at you.'

'Then why did you get rid of me so fast when the Bruntons came? Why didn't you ask me to stay just a little longer?'

'I nearly did.' His grin was rueful. 'Then I thought, this is crazy, you're up here to work, man, there goes your distraction. What are you thinking of, trying to stop her?'

'Your work, of course.' Of course his work always came first. 'And you got on so well after I'd gone.'

'I didn't get on at all after you'd gone.' Pattie gulped, then goggled listening to Duncan telling her unbelievably, 'I couldn't work for thinking of you and missing you and wanting you. I shifted tons of snow looking for that talisman of yours, that's what I did, and it kept on snowing and I never found the bloody thing. So then I thought I might as well get back down here. I hired one of Barney's men to keep digging, and I found it is possible for me to work so long as you're not too far away.'

'This isn't true,' she said, but if it was how wonderful it would be. 'If you followed me here why didn't you get in touch? If I hadn't gone to that exhibition——'

'I was waiting for your talisman. I wanted to bring it to you and say, "Remember me as well when you wear this." I didn't expect you at that exhibition. When you walked in I nearly grabbed you and held on to you, but I knew a photographer was around and I was far from sure you'd welcome being grabbed.'

'I would have done,' she said. 'Oh, I would!'

'You didn't show it. I was murderously jealous of Michael. I arranged for the carving to arrive that evening and hoped it would stir something.'

Her lips curved. 'You did? Well, it worked. But didn't you know that after the lodge I'd sort of lost interest in Michael?'

'You said that what happened at the lodge didn't count,' he reminded her, and she hated herself for her destructive defensiveness. She could have had this man, his loving, for long nights before this night. This was the last, and she would weep for the wasted ones. She wailed, 'Now you tell me, when you're going tomorrow!'

'Not without you.' He kissed her as she clung to him until the room started to swim around her. Then he said, 'If you hadn't come tonight I was coming for you. I can't do without you, I want you for good. Tomorrow we'll go and see a man about a wedding.'

'A *wedding*?' she echoed.

Duncan tilted her chin, a fist beneath it, smiling, but it was an uneasy smile, and he was pleading although he sounded masterful. 'I've had enough of waiting for you to make up your mind. This we do my way. We get married.'

'That should be fun,' Pattie said softly and shakily, and she saw the joy hit him and knew how much he must love her, and happiness blazed for her like a thousand stars.

'It will be,' he said. 'I promise you it will be. Fun and a whole lot more.'

'Will we live here?' She was whispering.

'Some of the time.'

'I'll like that,' she said. 'At least I think I will. But

I haven't seen it all yet. I haven't seen the rooms up there.' A staircase led to what had been the attics and now must be the bedrooms.

'You'll like them.' They stood so close, smiles stilled on their lips as passion rose to incredible intensity, and she slipped her arms around his neck, whispering again,

'I remember, there was a time you carried me upstairs.'

'I remember too,' said Duncan, and he lifted her, her heart thudding against his heart, and carried her, and as they reached the top of the stairs began to kiss her . . .

Harlequin Photo ❧Calendar❧

Turn Your Favorite Photo into a Calendar.

JULY 1984

The Browns

Uniquely yours, this 10x17½" calendar features your favorite photograph, with any name you wish in attractive lettering at the bottom. A delightfully personal and practical idea!

Send us your favorite color print, black-and-white print, negative, or slide, any size (we'll return it), along with 3 proofs of purchase (coupon below) from a June or July release of Harlequin Romance, Harlequin Presents, Harlequin Superromance, Harlequin American Romance or Harlequin Temptation, plus $5.75 (includes shipping and handling).

Harlequin Photo Calendar Offer
(PROOF OF PURCHASE)

NAME_____
(Please Print)

ADDRESS_____

CITY_____ STATE_____ ZIP_____

NAME ON CALENDAR_____

Mail photo, 3 proofs, plus check or money order for $5.75 payable to:	**Harlequin Books** P.O. Box 52020 Phoenix, AZ 85072	2-6

Offer expires December 31, 1984. (Not available in Canada)   CAL-1